THE OLD QUEEN'S TREASURE©

A Kohala Coast Thriller

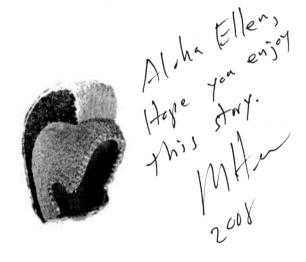

Aloha Ellen,
Hope you enjoy
this story.
MHerr
2008

by

Michael A. Herr

DISCLAIMER

This is a work of fiction. The characters are figments of my imagination. They don't exist! Any resemblance, except for actual historical figures, is purely coincidental. Locations and physical features of the island of Hawai`i may have been altered to fit the needs of my story.

* * * * * * * * * * * *

First Printing,

ISBN 978-1-4357-0991-1

Published by Lulu.com

Printing by InstantPublisher.com

Distributed in the United States by Booklines,
A division of The Islander Group

Printed in the United States of America

DEDICATION

To my ohana.
For family is, once you come down to it,
the most important thing of all.

A SPECIAL MAHALO PLENNY
To Penny Dunn, Wahine Maoli
For her assistance in proofreading this story.

FOREWORD

If you ever visit Mauana `Ala, the Royal Mausoleum up in Nu'uanu Valley on the island of O`ahu, and think that Queen Ka`ahumanu, the favorite wife of King Kamehameha, is resting there . . . you will be mistaken.

People will tell you that this is the Queen's final resting place . . . they are mistaken.

Yes, there is a body there. But the body is not that of Queen Ka`ahumanu.

The Queen rests elsewhere. She is at peace on the Big Island, not far from where her beloved husband Kamehameha also rests.

Both of them, reduced to the mana contained by their bones, lie hidden somewhere on the Big Island. Their locations are known only to a few. The guardians of the Queen's secret resting place are the women of a family that lives, and has lived for generations, along the Kohala Coast. They take their responsibility for guarding the hiding place of their Queen quite seriously.

Many others of royal birth are likewise buried throughout the Big Island. Other guardians watch over those burial places.

These burial places are sacred to the Hawai`ian people and ill be to those who would trespass there . . . and may even greater punishment befall those who remove those iwi, those sacred bones, or who steal the moepu, the personal items buried with these Hawai`ian ancestors.

The greatest punishment is reserved for someone who is Hawai`ian, whose family were children of this `aina, this land, and who breaks the traditions of his people to steal from either his own or other ancestors.

In short, do not disturb the sleep of the dead!

Ambition and Greed, like Pride
often go before a fall.

PROLOGUE
Kiholo Bay north of Kailua-Kona
Sunday, October 15, 2006

Somewhere deep under the waters of Kiholo Bay, below the bottom covering of muck and sand and rocks, deep within the bedrock pressed far beneath the ocean floor, forces straining against each other for years finally burst apart – freed from their state of impasse. The resultant release of energy traveled outward covering vast distances in virtually no time at all. At 7:08 a.m. this wave of energy struck the Big Island of Hawai`i. There the ground rolled and shook for fifteen seconds, though to the people on the island who experienced it the earthquake seemed to go on forever.

The tendrils of the earthquake stretched first to the north end of the island, rattling windows, knocking household items and store inventories from shelves. Ditches dug years ago high in the mountains were thrust into the air and broken, cutting off the life-giving water they brought to the fields below. Because it hit so early on a Sunday morning many people who otherwise might have been severely injured or even killed were spared any harm. Small rockslides that crashed down onto the roads did little more than block traffic and disrupt the daily routines of those living at that end of the island.

Afterward one man from the town of Hawi who was shaving told the story over and over of how his straightedge razor threatened to cut his throat as the bathroom floor shifted under his feet.

An instant after striking the northern end of the island the earthquake turned its attention to the area around Kawaihae . . .

* * *

Teri Maegher lay in her bed in San Francisco. Opening her eyes as the morning sun began to peek through the window she turned and looked at her husband Frank – lying so quiet and peaceful in bed next to her. Rolling over onto her side she softly reached out to stroke his face. Just before her fingertips brushed his cheek their bedroom shook violently. The king-size bed they shared split in two down the middle. Frank, isolated now, slid jerkily along with his half of the bed toward the window, while Teri, on her half, was bounced by the repeated shaking away from him and toward the opposite wall. Teri tried to call out to Frank but her throat closed tight with fear allowing not a single sound to escape. She reached out for Frank . . . managed to grab a piece of the blanket covering him . . . but the blanket slipped through her fingers and, even as she struggled to get out of her half of the bed in order to go to him, another violent shake sent Frank and his half of the bed bounding into the air and sailing out through the open window.

As if his departure freed her voice, Teri cried out in anguish . . . and awoke sitting up in her bed in her mother's house on the Big Island of Hawai`i far up the Kohala coast. Her bed still slid on its casters slowly around her bedroom – first one way, then the other. Her bedroom . . . the whole house in fact . . . shook and creaked. Teri gripped the covers and rode her bed like a surfboard caught in the chop from a passing motorboat. Without warning the shaking stopped. An unnatural silence filled the air. No morning birdsong at all.

Teri bolted from the bed and looked out the window. But Frank wasn't lying outside on his half of the bed. Instead all Teri saw outside was the too-bright beginning of another day.

Her memory of what had happened to Frank and where he now lay flooded back and forced Teri to her knees at the window. She sank slowly to the floor, turning until her back rested on the bedroom wall. A soft breeze flitted through the open window above her. It brought with it the sweet scent of plumeria. Faintly in the distance she could hear the sound of waves pounding on the shore of the Big Island. She remembered – she was in her family's old house on the Kohala coast. Leaning to one side she collapsed onto on the wood floor and, curling up, clasped her knees and sobbed.

She remembered! Everything!

Frank was dead. Her husband was gone from her – *forever*!

Far to the south in the town of Hilo, buffeted by nature many times over the years, church services had not yet begun in one small church. The congregation of that church who would have been struck by falling debris as they entered the church for services were instead simply jolted awake in their homes. As they gathered later that day at their church its damage reminded them about the fragility of life.

In the main hospital in Kona, ceiling panels and light fixtures rained down in the corridors. Fortunately no large influx of patients followed the heavy tremor although there was enough damage to close the hospital for that day and the next.

Somewhere between the main towns of Hilo and Kona just off Highway 11, the final blow of the earthquake, an aftershock of just slightly less intensity, struck a lava field. Below the smooth lava crust lay the Kazumura lava tubes, a series of tunnels created many hundreds of years ago and extending for miles beneath the surface. One section of one of the oldest lava tubes twisted slightly, much as a housewife might twist a dishtowel. A crack appeared in the wall of the tube. In the utter blackness of the tube nothing could be seen. Had there been even a spark of light it would have revealed, behind the crack in the wall, an old chamber. A chamber formed by a bubble in the lava over seven hundred years ago.

The earthquake subsided. In its wake it left behind the once-hidden chamber. And in the chamber three long-dead bodies – which, together with their secrets, were once more exposed to the world.

CHAPTER ONE
Kealakekua Bay, Hawai`i
December 1422

From his position on the east end of the top of the high cliff Kia`i looked down and to his left past the heiau of the priests to his village farther along the beach. There his sharp vision could identify each of the villagers as they went about their daily activities. Many had gone from the village earlier in the morning, out into the surrounding forest area to tend patches of taro and sweet potato.

Kia`i saw his wife sitting with a small group of women under the roof of an open-sided hut. His wife was using a cylindrical beater and stone anvil to give raw kapa bark its first beating. One day, Kia`i knew, his wife would be an expert at working with kapa and she would make the finest and thinnest kapa cloth for him to wear.

Looking down and to his right he could see, just as clearly, the large hale occupied by his chief, Pa`akiki. The chief's name was derived from his stubborn persistence as a child to outdo all others in all physical endeavors. Off to one side were two smaller hale belonging to the subchiefs. Off to the other side were two hale for the chief's wives and children. Set back within the tree line was a smaller hale used by the women for their monthly menstruation. All of the buildings were thatched with pili grass. But only the chief's hale was set upon a raised stone foundation. Kia`i had been allowed inside only twice before. Once when the chief assigned him to be a watchman for the village, and again when the chief had wished to hear his advice about the best way to guard the bay from attack. Both times were permanently engraved in Kia`i's memory due to the great honor each brought him. From those two ventures into the chief's hale Kia`i knew that the stone foundation, brought stone by stone down from the mountains, was covered with fine sand. And on top of the fine sand was a layer of thick lauhala mats, which, in turn, were covered with another layer of finer lauhala mats.

Kia`i saw that today two warriors were practicing wrestling in an area of soft sand in front of the chief's hut. They grappled with each other and tried out new holds as their friends looked on calling encouragement and advice, and sometimes made jokes about the warriors' efforts.

Kia`i raised his eyes and looked out over the wide blue sea as his duty commanded him. As his name declared, he was a watchman, a guardian of his village and his chief. Along with several others he spent a good part of each day gazing out to sea, making sure that no surprise attack was made upon the village. It was a duty, a responsibility, of utmost importance. It rested heavily on his shoulders, particularly since it was a duty given directly by his chief, Pa`akiki, himself. Kia`i glanced left at the sun. It was only slightly elevated. When he had taken over from the one who watched during the last part of the night the suns' arms had just begun to reach for the sky. The only items of interest on the sea right now were several canoes from the village. Kia`i knew the men who were out fishing and said a silent prayer for the success of their efforts and for their safety.

Seeing nothing on the horizon and no danger anywhere over the land, and knowing that, since it was Makahiki time, any approaching vessels would be more likely to bring friends than enemies, Kia`i stepped back from the cliff's edge, walked a short way along the trail behind him and propped his six-foot long thin spear made from heavy kauila wood against the trunk of a large kamani tree. Light grey punnai nuts hung heavy from the branches of the tree.

Perhaps I should take some of the nuts to my wife. She may need more of their oil for medicine. They might even soothe the itching on my thigh.

Kia`i's right hand moved down to his outer thigh, to the freshly tattooed design there. With effort he stopped himself from scratching, telling himself that in a day or two it would have healed enough for the itch to go away, but that to scratch right now might ruin the design. He would hate to do that after going through the painful procedure. It was a wonderful tattoo; a series of black triangles stacked one row on top of another and all leading to a four-line depiction of his aumakua, a pueo. Even as he had lain in the hut of the master canoe builder, who was also the most-sought-after tattoo artist, he had heard the call of an owl in the forest. To divert his thoughts from the itching Kia`i told himself to remember to pick some nuts from the tree later in the day before returning home. Stepping around the tree he walked three paces into the undergrowth. There he pulled aside his soft kapa malo and urinated long and satisfyingly. Regarding the ground in front of him, Kia`i decided that he would need to find a new area to urinate on for the next five or six days. This area was getting too damp and beginning to attract flies. Flicking the last drops of urine aside he readjusted his malo, picked up his spear from where it rested, and walked back out to his post on the top of the cliff. Kia`i stuck the butt of his spear into the ground to hold it and retrieved a water gourd from the shade behind a large boulder. As he raised the gourd to his lips to drink he suddenly froze in mid-motion.

Pouring a small amount of water into the palm of his hand Kia`i washed both his eyes. He focused his gaze on the far horizon. He blinked several times, rubbed his eyes lightly and once more looked toward the horizon.

He had not been mistaken. He saw an object, larger with every passing moment, rising above the horizon. The water gourd in his hand forgotten Kia`i concentrated all of his attention on the distant object.

Time passed as he watched the object grow in size. Eventually he was sure of two things; first that the object was unaccompanied, and second that it bore no resemblance to the war canoes of his people or those of the Tahitians, who had not traveled here for many generations. In fact, it was larger than the largest double-hull war canoe that Kia`i had ever seen. Its sails were different too, square rather than shaped like a crab's claw. Now that he was sure that the vessel was headed for the bay Kia`i put down the water gourd and picked up the large conch shell that was kept at the lookout.

Raising the shell to his lips Kia`i licked his lips, filled his lungs, and blew through the shell. The sound reached out over the bay to the hale at the far end, down to the chief's hale, and out to the workers in the forest. Kia`i filled his lungs again and blew a second time. He blew a third and final time and looked down to see the results of his signal.

In the village to his left people gathered at the shoreline to look out to sea, pointing excitedly. Further along the bay, midway between the village and the chief's hale, rose the heiau of the priests where they interpreted the signs of the heavens and offered sacrifices to the gods. Behind the heiau were their separate hale. Right now at the heiau the priests, standing on the top platform, were also looking out to sea, but without the unrestrained excitement demonstrated by the villagers. One of the priests had climbed to the top of the oracle tower for a better view and was calling down to his brethren in order to describe what he saw. A messenger quickly ran from the heiau along the hard-packed sand just above the surf line to tell the chief what the priest had seen, thus confirming the warning Kia`i had sounded.

Over to his right Kia`i noted that the chief along with his sub-chiefs and many of his warriors had gathered and were preparing to launch three of the large double-hull war canoes. The chief and all of his men had donned feathered war helmets and feathered capes along with lauhala mat waistbands. The chief carried a wooden lei o mano almost as long as a man's arm, inset with shark teeth on one end and sharpened to a point on the other. The priest messenger arrived and described what the other priests had seen from the top of the heiau. The chief listened and then gave the order to his men to launch the war canoes. Once launched they all made quick time rowing across the bay to the village. There, upon arrival, the chief drew his men around him, gave them instructions and then watched as his orders were carried out.

One group of heavily armed warriors under the direction of one of the sub-chiefs took up positions in hiding in the trees behind the villagers' hale. A few of the warriors moved among the villagers delivering instructions from the chief. As Kia`i watched men moved to the area where the imu for the men and women sat under a roofed open-sided shelter. They began quickly preparing the fire in each of the imu. Other men and women headed off to the forested area to gather fresh banana leaves for the imu along with food for the welcoming feast. Pa`akiki was a wise man and prepared for both a battle and a feast – the outcome would depend on the intentions of the new arrivals.

The chief along with his other sub-chief and the rest of the warriors formed up in seemingly careless array along the beach. But Kia`i noted that the warriors kept their hands on their weapons. With his keen eyesight Kia`i easily kept watch as the chief paced up and down on the beach continually casting his glance out to sea. The fact that Pa`akiki stood a good head taller than any other man in the village made him easy to pick out. The bright white lei niho pala`oa, a carving made from a whale's tooth and hung around the chief's neck by a cord braided from his own hair, made it doubly easy to do so. Kia`i knew that the lei niho held much of Pa`akiki's mana, mana that would be needed should battle be necessary. In battle warriors would seek not only to kill the chief, but would also seek to capture his lei niho pala`oa and thus also capture his mana, and by so doing add to their own power. Though it was the season of makahiki and warfare was generally forbidden, still these were strangers and one had always to be on guard. They would be greeted and a feast set out for them. But weapons would never be too far away from the eating utensils of the village's warriors.

CHAPTER TWO

Kia`i remained at his post. He was strongly tempted to race down the path that led to his village and the beach, but he knew his duty was not completed upon his signaling the arrival of the unknown vessel. There was always the possibility that this was a ruse, a distraction meant to focus all the village's attention in one direction while an attack was made from another direction. So he stayed. And he continued to watch the horizon in both directions as far as he could see in order to determine if the vessel entering the bay was accompanied by others who might attempt to land farther along the coast and attack the village overland.

* * *

From the top of the cliff Kia`i's keen eyesight allowed him to observe the strangers'arrival and their initial meeting with Pa`akiki. Upon entering the bay the strange vessel dropped all but one of its giant sails. Unusual sails they were, rectangular in shape rather than curved and tapering like the crab claw sails that Kia`i was so familiar with. The vessel itself was tall and angular with a myriad of ropes tied everywhere on it. While Kia`i recognized the purpose of many of the ropes, others puzzled him.

Kia`i watched the strange vessel roll slowly into the bay. When it was still farther than a sling could toss a stone the last sail was dropped and tied to the crosspiece while large stones tied to thick ropes were dropped into the water to anchor the vessel.

A flurry of activity aboard the strange vessel ended with two smaller craft being let down over the side. Men in garments more colorful than the kapa of the villagers quickly descended into these craft and began rowing toward shore.

Kia`i was so engrossed in watching this activity that he jumped in surprise when he heard a slight cough behind him. Turning he recognized his relief who would watch from now until the sun dipped below the horizon. Looking up Kia`i saw that the sun had moved directly overhead while he watched the arrival of the strange vessel. His watch finished for the day, Kia`i turned and quickly ran down the trail from the cliffs to the village. He paused only to pick a handful of nuts from the kamani tree. He wrapped them in a large leaf and shoved the bundle in between his malo and his hip.

* * *

Down at the beach and just in front of the village an historic meeting was taking place, though neither party realized it. The village chief, Pa`akiki, welcomed the strangers with words and gestures as they grounded their craft on the beach and stepped ashore. Their chief, easily recognized by the deference paid him by the others of his crew, replied with a burst of words that Pa`akiki did not know. But the strangers' chief also used some phrases resembling the Tahitian language of old. The two leaders could not have been more unalike. Pa`akiki was a giant of a man, deep brown of skin, with a broad nose, bright white teeth and curly black hair. His face was smooth, his hands large, his feet bare. Muscles rippled under his skin. In his younger days Pa`akiki had at times demonstrated his strength by crushing small coconuts in his hands.

The leader of the strangers had a much lighter complexion. In height he came barely to Pa`akiki's shoulder. Because of the silk robes that he wore it was not possible to see how muscled, if at all, he was. His feet were covered also rather than left bare. His hands were in proportion with his smaller size, but with long delicate fingers and long fingernails showing that he did little physical labor. He had a small goatee and a mustache that drooped down on either side of his mouth. His teeth though clean showed an addiction to something that tended to discolor them. The hair on his head was pulled straight back and plaited into a long braid. He wore a long sword in a sheathe on one hip and carried a dagger thrust through his belt at the other hip.

Slowly, through repetition and by the use of sign language, it became clear to Pa`akiki that the strangers wished to reprovision their ship. They had been on a long voyage and were headed home now, and were quite willing to trade for the provisions they needed.

Pa`akiki not only assured them that they were welcome to reprovision, but also that they were invited to a feast in the village that night. The strangers' chief indicated his thanks and acceptance of both offers.

* * *

Kia`i arrived down at the village just as the chief of the strange vessel began giving his men orders to proceed with reprovisioning their vessel. One group set off immediately in one of their small boats to return to their vessel. Those who remained on the beach stood watchfully around their second boat. Many attempts were made at communications and there was much interest on each side in the clothing and weapons of the other side. Kia`i expressed interest in a knife with a wooden handle carved in the shape of some fantastic creature's head that one of the landing party carried thrust thru his sash. He was disappointed when the other man would only let Kia`i look at the knife and would not let Kia`i hold it in his own hands.

Just as Kia`i was considering what he might offer the man in trade for the knife the small boat returned from the larger vessel. It was loaded with a number of cylindrical containers that, because the boat did not seem appreciably lower in the water, Kia`i judged to be empty.

The strangers' chief turned to one of his men, his sub-chief Kia`i guessed from his bearing, and barked out a series of commands. These did not appear to sit well with the sub-chief as he responded in a decidedly haughty manner. The strangers' chief drew himself up and yelled at his sub-chief so loudly that he drew the attention of even those villagers who were far away from the group on the beach.

With tight-drawn lips the sub-chief responded shortly and stomped off, as best as possible in the soft sand, to the boat with the empty containers.

"Kia`i," called Pa`akiki, "go with these strangers. Show them the stream where they may get fresh water."

"Yes, Pa`akiki," Kia`i replied as he set off after the strangers' sub-chief.

At first it seemed that the sub-chief might push Kia'i away, but with a friendly smile and gestures Kia'i made him understand that he was there to guide them to where they might fill their containers.

As Kia'i set off with the strangers in their boat toward the stream, Pa'akiki led the strangers' chief on a tour of the village. During his tour he introduced them to the village elders and the priests from the heiau further up the beach.

Shortly after being introduced to these strangers the priests left Pa'akiki and his guests and returned to the temple to say the appropriate prayers, make offerings to the gods, and seek divine information as to the purpose of the strangers. The men and women of the village set about the preparations for the feast.

Pa'akiki and the strangers' chief made themselves comfortable on a lauhala mat set in the shade of an open-sided hut where a number of men were at work building a new voyaging canoe. This construction gave Pa'akiki and the strangers' chief something in common to discuss – as best they could.

CHAPTER THREE

It was obvious to Kia`i that the strangers' sub-chief was furious. The man's jaw was clenched so tightly that Kia`i thought he might crack his own teeth. As the strangers' boat rode with the waves toward the beach below the cliffs the sub-chief continually squeezed his left hand into a fist while his right hand hovered over the knife that hung in a sheathe on his belt. Kia`i quickly gave up on his attempts to communicate with the man and concentrated instead on directing the oarsmen to where the freshwater stream ran down from the cliffs, crossed the beach, and joined the saltwater of the bay.

* * *

Other villagers were there by the freshwater stream when the strangers' craft, guided by Kia`i, grounded in the surf and was pulled ashore by its crew. Despite their curiosity the villagers kept to their tasks. Pa`akiki would expect everything to be in good order for the feast tonight, otherwise he would lose respect.

The strangers' sub-chief set his men to using smaller casks to fill the larger ones and his men soon had their routine for the work established. The sub-chief stood, hands on hips, watching the men for a short while. Then, satisfied that they could complete the task without his constant oversight, he walked away and back down the beach to where gentle waves broke over the rocks to fill tidepools.

* * *

Kang Pao's thoughts were full with fury. *To be addressed like that – berated even – in front of the men that I command . . . It's unthinkable! Besides, it wasn't my fault . . . not entirely . . . that the ship has been off-course for so long. And to threaten me with demotion! To be disgraced in front of all the crew.*

His hand moved to the haft of his knife again . . . but he knew better than to draw a weapon on the Captain. To do so would either mean that he died quickly here, or slowly when they returned to China. These thoughts did nothing to temper his anger.

Ahead of him were a series of tidepools. As he drew nearer Kang Pao observed that one of the pools, much larger than the others, was manmade. Just a little way away from this pool a native squatted on the beach grinding some nuts into powder on a flat stone. Intrigued Kang Pao watched as the man finished grinding the power, collected some of it in his hands and, stepping over to the large pool sprinkled the powder over the surface of the water. Kang Pao noticed now that there were a great many fish in the pool, most about as long as his hand. Obviously they had entered the pool at high tide and been trapped here when the tide receded. At first Kang Pao saw that the fish darted about, then they slowed, stopped, and floated to the surface. Of course! The ground nuts were a fish poison – quite similar to others he had seen on his many travels. But a very quick-acting poison. An idea began to form in Kang Pao's mind.

Shortly thereafter Kang Pao had determined, through sign language as usual with these savages, two things. One, that the poison would affect a man. Two, that for one small iron nail which he carried for just such a use, and whose properties Kang Pao demonstrated, the native was happy to provide Kang Pao with a large quantity of the powdered poison.

Kang Pao wrapped the poison in his silk handkerchief, tucked it in a pocket of his pants and, with a smile on his face now, set off back up the beach to check on the progress of his work party.

* * *

When all the casks were filled and re-sealed, Kang Pao led his work party back to the treasure ship leaving Kia`i at the steam to find his own way back down the beach.

Once back on the treasure ship, and after directing the work party to bring the filled casks back onboard, and to fill the small boat with more empty casks, Kang Pao slipped below deck.

Alone in his cabin Kang Pao set his silk handkerchief which contained the poison on top of the small table that was secured to the floor in the middle of his cabin. *What if it is so bitter that he rejects it?* Steeling himself Kang Pao licked the tip of his finger and touched it to the pile of poison. His wet finger captured a few granules of the poison and he now brought his finger back to his mouth. *Bitter . . . but not so bitter that he will notice it mixed in with his dinner.*

Kang Pao put a third of the poison onto a piece of paper that he then folded into a small packet. He hid the packet in a pocket of his clothing where it would be easily accessible to him. He guessed that a third of the poison would do for his purposes. The rest of the poison he rewrapped in his silk handkerchief and hid among his personal effects. Climbing back up on deck Kang Pao directed his work party during two more trips over to the freshwater stream.

After the final trip Kang Pao debased himself by apologizing profusely to the Captain who had returned to the ship. Kang Pao entreated the Captain to allow him to accompany him to the planned feast in the native village. The Captain grudgingly agreed to allow Kang Pao to accompany him to the feast.

Kang Pao went below to clean himself and put on fresh clothes. He transferred the poison packet to the pocket of the new pants he wore. As he finished dressing one of the crew knocked discreetly on his door to inform him that the Captain was preparing to leave for the feast on shore. Before leaving to join the Captain and the rest of the party going ashore Kang Pao checked his appearance in the small mirror hung by his bunk. The smile he practiced was genuine and brought about by his thoughts as to the outcome of tonight's feast.

CHAPTER FOUR

As the sun dropped below the horizon men from the village pulled back the covering from both the men's imu and the women's. Li Fong, the Captain of the Emperor's treasure ship now at anchor in the bay of this uncharted island looked on with mild interest. In his voyages he had often seen similar cooking methods. From the two imu the natives retrieved baskets of vegetables, among which he recognized sweet potatoes. Fish had also been steamed in one of the imu along with three dogs. Eating dog did not bother Li Fong; especially since the village chief had shown him how the dogs that were intended to be eaten were first fed a diet of vegetables in order to make their flesh more palatable. After all, he had eaten many other strange and, sometimes, delicious creatures during the ship's voyage.

Following the native chief's beckoning Li Fong went to join him on one of a number of large mats placed on a large open area between the native huts. Tonight the men's eating house was not used, though the women ate in their eating house. These strangers were very different from anyone else Pa`akiki had ever known and so he chose to feast with them out in the open. Lowering himself down onto the mat, after adjusting his sword and dagger, Li Fong waved his own men over to join the native feast. He had allowed only a few of his men to partake of this feast. After so much time at sea and so many encounters with savages in strange lands Li Fong had learned to be extremely careful. Most of his men remained on board the junk, and of those men half stood guard while half slept above deck.

Kang Pao sat down next to Li Fong. As First Mate it was appropriate for him to occupy that seat. Li Fong frowned at his First Mate briefly before letting his face go blank again. His first thought had been to deny Kang Pao the opportunity to feast on fresh food. But Kang Pao had apologized most profusely and had bowed so low in obeisance that Li Fong had felt obliged to bring him to the feast. Not that his mind had changed. When they returned to China Li Fong would see to it that Kang Po's star no longer rose in the sky. If he had anything to say about it – and he did – Kang Po would never set sail under the Emperor's banner again.

* * *

The feast progressed well and the abundance of food presented to the guests brought great honor to Pa`akiki. After all seated had eaten their fill from the wooden platters that were passed around, the evening's entertainment began. Young men and women from the village arrived and danced hula accompanied by a variety of drum and gourd instruments. As the dancing increased in vigor the drink of the feast was brought out. Awa, strong indeed, was poured into coconut shell cups and passed to the revelers.

Kang Pao took the cup of awa intended for his Captain, but before passing it on he drew the Captain's attention to the antics of a very large older woman who had joined the dancers and was now doing a comic, and quite ribald, version of the dance performed earlier by the younger dancers. While Li Fong and the native chief laughed and nudged each other in appreciation of the older woman's dance efforts, Kang Pao retrieved the paper packet of fish poison from his pocket and surreptitiously poured a large measure of the poison into Li Fong's drink. He stirred it quickly with his finger.

The bitter taste of the awa hid the taste of the fish poison somewhat. Li Fong knew better than to reject the drink, especially when Pa`akiki tilted back his head and finished off his entire cupful and then looked expectantly at Li Fong. Immediately that he had emptied his cup Pa`akiki signaled a young native man to bring over a gourd of awa and refill all their cups.

Before starting on his second cup of awa Li Fong reached behind him and brought forward something wrapped in cloth. Extending the parcel in both his hands he presented it to Pa`akiki. Smiling, Pa`akiki bowed in gratitude. He unwrapped the parcel to disclose a blue and white porcelain platter. Pa`akiki was delighted with the gift. The porcelain was a material he had never seen. It reminded him somewhat of lava . . . but he could not imagine anyone being able to fashion lava into a platter. He placed the platter on the cloth in front of him, again expressed his appreciation, and urged the others to enjoy their cups of awa.

Li Fong smiled behind his cup at his ability to manipulate people and situations. As example, an inexpensive platter from the galley had just gained him great respect from these savages.

The feasting and entertainment continued until the moon was quite high in the sky. Before that time however Li Fong felt his guts twist into knots and he was forced to leave the feast area to find somewhere to relieve himself. He wasn't quite in time.

Forced to clean himself, and his undergarments, with leaves from some plants close at hand, Li Fong made his way back to the feast. He walked doubled over with gut-wrenching pain. He clutched his stomach as if to hold his intestines in place. With great difficulty he forced himself to stand upright in order to thank Pa`akiki and then he all but ran to his own boat. Cursing his men to give their utmost Li Fong rushed from the small boat up the rope ladder and down to his own chambers at the rear of the junk. His relief when he located his chamber pot was short-lived as another bout of pain struck almost immediately.

* * *

Leaning against the wall with his ear close to the door Kang Pao smiled at the sounds of the Captain's obvious distress.

CHAPTER FIVE

The knock on his door roused the Captain from the most horrible night he had ever spent aboard ship. He lay on his side, his knees pulled up to his chest, his braid loosened and glistening with sweat. The knock came again.

"Who's there?" he tried to shout in impatience, but fatigue made his voice barely audible outside.

"Kang Pao, sir, I have brought something to ease your discomfort."

"One moment," Li Fong replied. With effort he forced himself up and out of bed. Seeing the awful mess from the previous night he set about wiping up the most frightful-looking areas with his already-soiled garments. Tossing everything into a pile in the far corner of the room he slowly made his way to his table, bolted to the floor, and its accompanying chair. Once seated he called out to Kang Pao to enter.

"Good morning, Captain. I hope you are feeling better after your . . . unpleasant reaction to last night's feast."

Li Fong only grunted in reply.

Kang Pao slid a large bowl, covered with a cloth, onto the table in front of the Captain.

"I asked the cook to prepare this especially for you. It should ease your . . . discomfort."

The Captain made a noise of appreciation, or perhaps it was his stomach again.

"Thank you for your concern. I shall have it later."

"Oh, but sir, if I may, the heat of this soup," and Kang Pao lifted the cloth to reveal a steaming bowl of broth, "will certainly ease your stomach. Why, the cook swears that within a short time of finishing this you will be your old self again. Please, Captain, eat. We need you strong in order to finish the reprovisioning so that we may return to our homeland."

Persuaded by his own desire to show strength rather than weakness, Li Fong took the spoon that Kang Pao extended to him. He began to eat the heavily seasoned soup.

Kang Pao stood and watched until the Captain finished the bowl. Bowing slightly he retrieved the soup, spoon and cloth and backed out the door.

After returning the items to the galley and reminding other crew members that the Captain was not feeling well and desired to be left alone so that he could rest, Kang Pao went quietly back to stand briefly outside the door to the Captain's quarters. The sounds from inside brought a broad smile to his face.

CHAPTER SIX

Li Fong remained in his cabin all that day. In the evening Kang Pao returned to check on his Captain's welfare. He brought news that the reprovisioning efforts were going well and that they should be completed by the middle of the day tomorrow. He also brought another bowl of soup from the cook.

"He swears on the head of his favorite mistress that this soup will do what the morning soup obviously was unable to do," Kang Pao spoke in a soft voice, a reassuring voice that one would use with a very ill patient.

Li Fong required assistance to his chair and Kang Pao had to put the spoon in his hand and help lift the first spoonful of soup to his mouth. So close to the Captain, Kang Pao worked to keep from breathing in the stench that filled the room. As Li Fong struggled with this new bowl of soup Kang Pao observed the bloody detris strewn about the room. Even the sheets of the bed were soaked with fecal matter and blood. Standing behind Li Fong and out of his line of sight, Kang Pao smiled with great satisfaction.

CHAPTER SEVEN

In the morning it was Kang Pao who found the Captain dead in his cabin. His expressions of grief were masterfully demonstrated. Soon after the news had spread to all crewmembers, Kang Pao announced his elevation to Captain of the Emperor's junk. Since he had been First Mate this increase in rank was treated as natural by all the crewmembers. To do otherwise could bring accusations of mutiny.

Kang Pao decreed, and was supported in his decision by the Captain's physical appearance, that the Captain's body should be buried here on this uncharted island rather than being carried back to his homeland. Several of the lowest crew members were brought in to help wrap the Captain's body and to thoroughly clean Kang Pao's new quarters. Unfortunately, fears of contagion forced Kang Pao to raise his voice quite a bit in order to get both these tasks completed. As it was, the men worked exceedingly quickly and wore improvised silk masks, which were heavily perfumed to combat the stench of the chamber.

* * *

At first Pa`akiki seemed to be living up to his name and his reputation for stubbornness once more, but then he relented and agreed to allow the strangers' chief to be buried here. His agreement was somewhat influenced by the demonstration of the firing of a cannon on the strangers' vessel. It took only three shots for the crew of the junk to blow apart an empty cask they had set floating in the bay.

Changing his mind, Pa`akiki made it clear to the strangers that so high-ranking a leader as their chief appeared to be deserved only the best of burial sites. The best site, however, was quite a distance away from the village. He did not mention the fears of the villagers, and himself, as to what the ghost of this stranger might do if he was buried close to the village.

Thus it was that a mixed procession set out the following morning over the hills. Six members of the junk's crew took turns by two's carrying the body of the late Captain wrapped in his finest silk robe and suspended from a pole. An equal number of warriors from the village carrying gourds with smoldering fire inside and torches formed from bamboo tubes and oily kukui nuts walked ahead of the pallbearers. Kia`i had asked Pa`akiki if he might be part of the burial party, due in large part to his curiosity over these strangers. He pointed out that he had assisted the stranger who now seemed to have taken over leadership of the strangers' group. Pa`akiki agreed. Now Kang Pao and Pa`akiki, along with the others of the party, accompanied the late Captain on his final journey. Pa`akiki cast curious glances now and then at the wrappings that held the body of the strangers' chief. He wondered at their burial customs and whether or not the bundle contained only the stripped long bones and skull of the man as his own religion required. Shrugging, he thought to himself that these strangers had very odd customs.

* * *

After several hours of walking the group arrived at a fairly large black cave-like opening in the earth. While Kang Pao's men set their burden down and rested, Pa`akiki's men set about lighting their torches. One of the chief's warriors, holding his torch aloft, led the group down into what Kang Pao quickly discerned to be a roundish tube of hard smooth black rock that, at times, almost resembled glass. As they moved further into the tube Kang Pao was able to see in the flickering light of the torches striations, bands of color on the walls. He guessed that these bands had been deposited over the years. The bands differed in width as much as they did in color. Even in the poor lighting provided by the torches Kang Pao could discern bands of red, yellow, brown and blue. *It's all quite beautiful,* he thought even as a part of his mind cringed under the massive weight of the earth above.

CHAPTER EIGHT

The walk was long and difficult. Try as he might Kang Pao could not keep track of the route they followed. He sincerely hoped that the savages could find their way out again.

Without warning the native chief called a halt. He told his men to remain where they were, took a torch from one man and, beckoning, led Kang Pao and the two men carrying Li Fong's body down a side tunnel. They had not gone very far when the native chief bent down and disappeared from Kang Pao's sight. Stepping carefully ahead Kang Pao found a smaller roundish tunnel opening in the wall of the main tunnel. Kang Pao followed the light of the native chief's torch into the smaller tunnel. The ceiling in this tunnel was so low that he was forced to duck his head low and walk with his knees deeply bent. Then the tunnel made an abrupt turn while also narrowing down so much that he was forced to bend almost double while pulling his arms in close to his sides. Not very far along the small tunnel opened up again into an almost-round cavern with extremely smooth walls. At the back of this bubble chamber the lava had formed a sort of natural altar. The native chief stood in the center of the cavern looking around at the walls. He indicated that this was the place where they would leave Li Fong's body.

Kang Pao summoned the two crewmen bearing Li Fong's corpse. With some effort they manhandled their burden through the narrow tunnel and into the bubble chamber. Kang Pao directed them to place the silk-wrapped body on a level portion of the floor to the right of the natural lava rock altar. Immediately after completing their task one of the men, eyes wide in the flickering light of the torch held by the native chief, scrambled back out of the cavern. The native chief looked at Kang Pao and said something in his own language that Kang Pao chose to interpret as "Will this do?" Kang Pao nodded and stepped toward the opening of the cavern. Pausing he looked down at

Li Fong's body one more time. Showing an unexpected burst of emotion Kang Pao stepped over to the body, pulled a blue and white porcelain platter wrapped in a piece of silk out of a cloth bag he had been carrying all day. The platter was identical to the one Li Fong had gifted Pa`akiki with. They were both everyday platters from the galley of the treasure ship. He placed the platter at Li Fong's feet, reached again into the bag and brought forth three pieces of fruit, just beginning to show signs of rotting, that he set on the platter.

"Here is a little nourishment for your long trip into the afterworld," Kang Pao said loudly enough that the rest of his men outside could hear him. Not to give food to Li Fong's ghost might have led to unwanted speculation by his crew. Kang Pao smiled as he congratulated himself on his ability to have others see what he wanted them to see.

Nodding to the native chief he hastened to exit the chamber, leaving behind only the chief and one of his own seamen.

Pa`akiki looked at the last stranger left in the bubble chamber with him. The man reached under his shirt and produced a knife whose handle was carved in the shape of a strange animal with horns and whiskers. Pa`akiki tensed, shifted one foot back and prepared to use the flaming torch to defend himself. The stranger regarded the chief for a moment before turning to the wrapped body on the floor of the chamber. Stepping over to the body he lifted part of the wrappings and placed the knife on the corpse's chest.

"You always treated me fairly, Captain. It's only right that you have something to defend yourself with in the next life. Safe voyage to you." And with those words, none of which Pa`akiki understood, the man stooped and entered the narrow tunnel to rejoin his crewmates and his new Captain.

Pa`akiki relaxed as the man disappeared down the narrow tunnel. Taking one more look around at the burial chamber and its new occupant, Pa`akiki also set off down the entry tunnel.

Once outside he gave the command for the group to begin its return journey to the village.

CHAPTER NINE

Standing at the rail of his ship watching the island disappear behind him Kang Pao smiled broadly. He was master of the treasure ship now. No one disputed him in that claim. Once they returned home and gave the emperor his portion of the goods they had collected, Kang Pao would receive the largest share, the Captain's share, of the treasure.

Going below to his new quarters Kang Pao pulled out the ledger in which the details of their voyage were recorded. He read the Captain's last entry and then sat staring at the blank pages following that entry. Eventually he picked up a thin brush and wrote the entry for their time on the island.

"Chanced upon an uncharted island. Reprovisioned the boat with fresh water from a stream along a beach. Caught a good number of green sea turtles, which we are keeping alive on deck in order to provide us with fresh meat on the journey home.

Captain Li Fong became quite ill with some type of island fever and after a brief illness died. In order to avoid having other members of the crew becoming ill, the Captain was buried on the island. I, as First Mate, assumed command of the vessel. We departed to continue our voyage home in order to deliver to the Emperor the goods that we have acquired."

Kang Pao did not bother to include any information as to the location of the island, nor did he describe the location where Li Fong was buried.

Yes, Kang Pao was very pleased.

CHAPTER TEN
Just before Makahiki, 1426

After many years gazing out over the ocean in order to assure that neither enemy nor friend arrived unnoticed Kia`i's eyes began to fade. Fearing what might become of him should he no longer be able to fulfill his responsibility at some time in the future, and seeing that his wife, somewhat older than he, had still not recovered fully from the difficult birth of their only son three years ago, Kia`i gave his son to his uncle and aunt to be hanai. They agreed readily to raise the boy as their own. The uncle and aunt lived away from the village, up toward the mountain, and there they grew much taro and other crops for the village below. Kia`i and his wife saw their son often as he grew. They were very proud of him.

About the time that their son was ten years old, Kia`i's wife, Lau'ohonani, died peacefully in her sleep. Kia`i used a length of rope wrapped around her neck and passed under her knees to pull her body into a more rounded shape. He then wrapped her in kapa, a fine piece that she had made herself. With the help of two of the women that she had worked closely with Kia`i carried her body farther down the coast to a sandy area that the two of them had visited often. There she was buried, close enough to the ocean that her spirit could look out over the blue water forever.

CHAPTER ELEVEN
Very late in the Year, 1449

Not long after his wife's death, Kia`i could no longer see even the closest sail approaching the village. Because of his years of service to his chief Kia`i was given another responsibility. He was given the opportunity to assist the adze maker. Since he had come to this activity late in life Kia`i lacked the skill to chip rock correctly. So Kia`i was allowed to assist by doing some of the rougher grinding of blades and was also responsible for fastening the finished blade to a wooden haft. Sometimes, in the heat of the afternoon, Kia`i fell asleep sitting in the shade of the shelter in which he worked beside the other craftsmen.

However Kia`i did his best working at this new job and over the years gained some small measure of skill at the things he did.

While dozing sitting up one afternoon Kia`i was jolted awake by cries of lamentation. Standing up and moving into the bright sunlight, which caused him to shade his now milky eyes, Kia`i asked the others what was happening. He was informed that Pa`akiki had died during his sleep, a fact that his second wife had just discovered. Not an unexpected death, for the chief had been ill for months, but a disturbing event in any case. Kia`i joined with the rest of the village in making his way around the bay to the chief's hale. There, he and the others sat in the sand listening to the cries of Pa`akiki's wives and children. Off to one side Pa`akiki's nephew, Kaneloa, so named because he was even taller than his uncle though not as strong, knowing that he would soon be chief, respectfully mourned his uncle even while covertly eyeing his uncle's house and possessions.

The priests came from the temple and, chanting, directed the removal of Pa`akiki's body, wrapped in banana, taro and paper mulberry leaves. The priests carried the body, followed by the mourning members of the chief's family and the villagers, back to the men's eating-house. There, in a far corner, they dug a shallow grave and kindled a fire over the body. For the next ten days the fire was kept burning while the priests took turns chanting beside the body. At the end of that time the entire village gathered once more to bear witness as the body was removed from the burning pit. The priests removed the remaining flesh from the bones, wrapped it in a bundle of fresh banana leaves and gave the bundle to the chief's nephew. Kaneloa, together with several warriors, reverently carried the bundle to a canoe and pushed off. They paddled far out beyond the breakers at the mouth of the bay. Once far out to sea Kaneloa, with appropriate chants, deposited these remains of his uncle in the ocean. With that duty completed he and his men headed back for shore.

In the meantime the priests had finished preparing the skull, the long leg bones and the arm bones of Pa`akiki for burial. The rest of his bones were taken away by two of the priests for burial far past the end of the beach. A sennit casket that the chief's women had woven over the past ten days was brought forward and Pa`akiki's bones and skull were positioned as if the old king was sitting in the casket. The top of the small casket was fastened on with other strips of sennit and the casket was then placed on a raised area. The head priest knelt in front of the casket and prayed while the entire village knelt behind him on the sand.

* * *

With the ceremonies in the village completed Kaneloa selected those who would form a burial procession for his uncle. Kia`i knelt before Kaneloa and pleaded with him to be allowed to accompany his chief one last time. With misgivings Kaneloa agreed to his request.

CHAPTER TWELVE

Though he gave his every effort, Kia`i still fell many times during the long journey to the selected burial site for Pa`akiki. His vision was so poor by now that he could not adequately see the path that the procession followed. At least he was not burdened, as most of the others were, with moepu, the possessions of the chief that would accompany him on his journey into the next world. Along with the casket containing Pa`akiki's bones the procession bore two canoe paddles and a one-person canoe with outrigger, several of his best spears, a number of carefully crafted bone fishhooks, the sharks tooth lei o mano with which he had met the strangers many years before, his own whale's tooth lei niho pala`oa in which resided so much of his mana, a bamboo flute that he had learned to play with some success, a large calabash that would hold his food in the next world, his feather helmet and feather cape, the platter that years ago the leader of the strangers from the large odd vessel had given him as a gift and, lastly, wrapped in a piece of soft kapa, the chief's own personal feathergod.

After many hours of walking with only a few short breaks the procession reached the entrance to a vast underground labyrinth of lava tubes. Kukui nut torches were taken out of lauhala sacks and were soon lit. With the torches illuminating the tube walls the procession carefully entered the lava tube.

* * *

To Kia`i's eyes the torches were only bright dots in the darkness. He would have fallen continually had not one of the priests taken pity on him and taken hold of his elbow to guide him.

They walked for an unknown amount of time and took so many twists and turns that Kia`i would never have been able to find his way back. But that did not matter to him.

Eventually, off to their right they came upon a roundish opening in the main lava tube. Setting torches in cracks in the tube wall the men doubled over and scuttled like crabs into the smaller tube. Fortunately the journey through this tube was not so long. At the other end they came out in a large bubble chamber, formed when lava on an earlier eruption had first pushed in and then flowed back out. The interior of this chamber was very smooth and at the back a natural altar had been formed in the lava. Off to one side of the altar lay a body wrapped in soft robes – the leader of the strangers who had stopped here so many years ago.

Having accompanied Pa`akiki on a journey to this chamber many years ago Kia`i did not need his eyes to tell him what lay here. Kia`i held a torch aloft and stood off to one side as the priests arranged Pa`akiki's casket on the natural altar and placed around it the items they had brought to provide for him in the next world. The last item they placed was the representation of Pa`akiki's god. The god-statue had been made by Pa`akiki himself from a thick piece of a root from a kukui nut tree. Pa`akiki had caught many little birds in the forest using a sticky sap and had carefully plucked a few feathers from each bird before cleaning off the sap and releasing the bird. The bright feathers he applied all around the god-statue except for the top of the head. There he used dark black feathers to represent hair. He added shells for eyes and finished the representation off with a cruel mouth fitted all around with pointed dogs' teeth. When the priests had finished the arrangements they prayed and chanted for a short time, their voices resounding strangely in the hollow chamber.

One by one those in the burial chamber made their way back out the smaller entry tunnel. Soon only the high priest and Kia`i remained in the burial chamber.

"It is time to leave, Kia`i," said the priest.

"I shall remain here with my chief."

"You know that we must seal this entrance."

"I know. I will stay with Pa`akiki. Very soon now I shall be with him in the next world. I pray that I may continue to serve him there."

The high priest sighed, but saw that Kia'i's way was best. The man was old and nearly blind. He was of little use to the village anymore and would surely die soon. Here he could fulfill a greater destiny than any he could achieve now back at the village.

"As you wish."

* * *

As soon as the high priest exited the entry tunnel to the burial chamber the warriors began to backfill the tunnel with lava rock they had collected while the priests had been praying. Inside the chamber Kia'i ducked back as the first few lava rocks bounced inside as they were tossed into the entry tunnel from outside. Soon the rocks piled up in the entry tunnel and blocked it. The final lava rocks were placed more carefully to fill up the entry to the tunnel. Then powder from crushed rocks was mixed with water that had been brought in gourds. This mixture was used to fill all the cracks in the rocks blocking the entry. When the men were finished the opening of the entry tunnel was no longer visible in the light from the torches.

Gathering up their belongings the group turned and began making their way back to their village.

Kaneloa led them out of the lava tube into the sunlight. He paused just outside the entrance to the lava tube.

As the others passed by him he called out to the high priest, "Where is the man Kia'i?"

"He remains with your uncle, as his servant and guardian in the next world." The high priest continued along the path to the village.

Kaneloa looked back down the black tube and shivered.

* * *

In the burial chamber his torch was slowly flickering and dying, as he himself was.

Kia'i curled up on the floor of the chamber just in front of the altar. He did not feel the cold. He looked up at the casket containing Pa'akiki's bones. He looked up at Pa'akiki's feathered god. As he closed his eyes for the last time Kia'i could have sworn that through the dimness he saw not a frown, but a smile on the face of the feathered god.

* * *

The last of the warriors in the procession paused to look back at the black lava cavern. In his mind he pictured Kia`i alone in the dark. A tear ran down his cheek to wind up in the corner of his mouth. He tasted its saltiness.

As he gazed back at the cavern an owl came gliding silently out of the blackness. It landed on the branch of a tree beside the trail and looked down at the warrior. Then it pushed off and followed the rest of the group along the path back to the village.

Kia`i's son followed the pueo; his faith telling him that it was his aumakua, his father now watching over him.

CHAPTER THIRTEEN
University of Beijing
May 29, 2006

The characters on the small bronze plaque on the door told the visitor that this was the office of Professor Chao Bai, Head of the University's Department of Archeology and Anthropology. Assistant Professor Hwang Tam paused outside the door, wiped his palms on the sides of his pants, rotated his head first to the right and then to the left, shrugged his shoulders, cleared his throat and knocked smartly on the door.

"Come in."

The office was moderately large and furnished well. Shelving on both sides of the office held a multitude of books of all sizes – some new and many old. Along with the books the shelves were occupied with pottery, weaponry, utensils and strange objects collected over many years by the Professor. Having been to the Professor's office before, Hwang Tam knew that the wall behind him displayed an extensive collection of masks from many countries along with photos of the Professor in the company of numerous exalted officials.

Professor Chao Bai's desk backed up to the window wall behind him. Outside the window bright sunshine spilled over the campus and warmed the many students walking to and from classes. The positioning of the window and the desk also forced his visitors to squint in order to see the Professor.

Professor Chao Bai stood up and came around from behind his highly polished rosewood desk. He was shorter than Hwang Tam and while he still had a full head of hair, that hair was entirely white now. Nevertheless, he radiated a self-assurance that Hwang Tam could only wish he might some day attain. The Professor bowed slightly to Hwang Tam, who, in return, bowed much more deeply.

With a gesture of his right hand Professor Chao Bai indicated that Hwang Tam should take a seat in the chair facing the Professor's desk. Hwang Tam sat on the edge of the chair, back erect and his right hand shoved firmly into his right jacket pocket.

From his high-backed leather chair behind the desk the Professor stared at Hwang Tam as he would at a recently unearthed clay pot – with both recognition of the nature of the pot and some slight curiosity as to how it might be useful to him.

The Professor placed his elbows on his desk and steepled the fingers of both hands together.

"So, you have everything prepared for your departure tomorrow?"

"Yes, Professor. My bags are packed, my passport and visa are in order . . . and my arm may even stop aching by then from the shots that the nurse gave me."

The men laughed lightly together, both at one time or another having suffered under the ministrations of Nurse Gao in the University's antiseptic clinic.

"This is a great opportunity for you," Professor Chao Bai continued, his voice dropping to emphasize the seriousness of his remarks. "I hope you will treat it appropriately."

Hwang Tam bowed his head in acknowledgement of the good fortune he had received.

"I shall make every effort to do so," he replied.

"You are the first member of our department to receive a scholarship to study with members of the Archeology Department at Stanford University. Many of your colleagues would give much to change places with you."

Again Hwang Tam bowed his head. But he did not interrupt his Department Chair.

"I assume that you will also use this coming year abroad to continue your . . . efforts?"

Hwang Tam knew exactly what Professor Chao referred to, and deliberated for a moment before responding.

"Only on my own time, Professor." Then, unable to resist, he went on, "This year-long sabbatical does provide me with a great opportunity to search for proof to my theory. As you know, only recently I uncovered a logbook from one of the Emperor's treasure ships. There is much missing from this logbook due both to its age and also to incomplete entries. But I believe, from my interpretation of those entries, that at some point this ship and crew set foot on the New World. Years before Columbus! It is even possible that on their return voyage to China the ship put in on the Hawai`ian islands."

During his impassioned speech Hwang Tam had leaned further and further forward in his chair. His eyes widened and the zeal he felt was revealed in them.

Chao Bai cocked his head slightly but did not bother to get into a discussion on this point with Hwang Tam. In his own mind he noted that the theory was not Hwang Tam's alone. Many were of the belief that China, during the period of the Ming Dynasty and by command of the Emperor Zhu Di, had explored much farther than was generally acknowledged by most scholars. Hwang Tam was but one of that group. Hwang Tam went further than most and believed fully that the Chinese expeditions had reached the Americas long before Columbus in his puny vessels had sighted land there.

"Yes, it is," was all Chao Bai said. He stood up. "Well, I wish you good fortune. I sincerely hope that you bring honor to this Department with your studies at Stanford University. Have you been told yet which professor you will work with?"

Calmer now, Hwang Tam stood also. "Yes, Professor. I have been assigned to Professor Thompson. He has done much work on both Native Americans and indigenous peoples. There is an assistant professor who I will work with also. An American woman, Felicia Cardinale. I hope to learn much from the professor. And of course, I hope to be able to find irrefutable proof of my theory while in America."

"I believe that I met Professor Thompson at a conference once," Chao Bai replied ignoring Hwang Tam's hope to find proof of his theory. "Professor Thompson seemed quite . . . capable. You may mention my name to him if you wish," and Professor Chao Bai rose smoothly from his chair.

Out of habit the Professor started to reach across his desk to shake hands at the conclusion of their meeting. Smoothly he changed direction and brought his hand up to smooth back his already perfectly combed hair before bringing both hands down to hang at his side.

The two men bowed to each other and Hwang Tam stepped to the door. Grasping the knob in his left hand he pulled the door open.

"Good fortune, Assistant Professor Hwang. I wish you success."

Hwang Tam bowed once more before stepping through the door and closing it behind him. He stood outside the door picturing the office inside . . . but slightly changed, his name on the brass plaque on the desk, pictures of him on the walls beside his diplomas, framed newspaper articles attesting to his greatness.

And when I succeed my success will bring me the title of Professor . . . along with your position here at the University.

Hwang Tam smiled at the thought.

* * *

Before sitting back down and tackling one of the mountains of work on his desk Chao Bai entertained his own thoughts – *What a foolish quest. Still, if by some miracle he were to succeed, how much more respect from my colleagues would I gain from his efforts! Perhaps . . .*

Chao Bai opened his desk drawer, withdrew a pack of unfiltered cigarettes and shook one out of the pack. He retrieved a lighter from the same drawer, lit the cigarette and replaced both the lighter and the pack of cigarettes in the drawer before closing it. Leaning back in his chair he inhaled deeply, held the smoke in his lungs for a brief period and then blew a smoke ring toward the ceiling of his office. Chao Bai allowed his mind to drift off into the realm of possibilities as a smile blossomed on his face.

CHAPTER FOURTEEN
Somewhere in the Kazumura Lava Tubes
February 6, 2007

The two men shuffled along through the pitch-blackness of the lava tube – their way illuminated only by the dim pools of light thrown ahead of them by their cheap flashlights. The light was not enough to keep them from regularly bumping various parts of their bodies on the rough floor and walls of the tube. The man leading was tall and large, enough so that he was forced to walk slightly stooped over to avoid striking his head on the ceiling. He moved with a deliberate step, his feet at times crushing some of the lava rocks beneath them. Following him was a lean short man who moved in a more jittery style, flitting from side to side of the tube and thus injuring himself more often than the bigger man. The two men were dressed similarly; baggy board shorts, overly large tee shirts, and old scuffed boots. Neither wore socks but both had loosely tied the shoestrings of the boots, so as to prevent tripping on them. The temperature inside the lava tube, in the low sixties, along with the water that often dripped onto them from the ceiling as they walked along, made them shiver frequently. Both men had several minor cuts and scrapes on their legs from encounters with jagged lava protrusions.

"Hey, for da las' time . . . NO! No money!"

"Come on, Lalepa, I'm busted. I lost big on the Superbowl . . . an' it's not like Billy Ng going to go all soft an' let me off the hook. An' my girlfriend – "

"Screw her! Fact, more better you screw her den screw wit' Billy. You know what Billy do wit' guys who don' pay him what dey owe?"

Lalepa's partner waved his left hand in general dismissal of Lalepa's comments. It would have been a more dramatic gesture had

Lalepa been able to see it in the darkness of the lava tube they were traversing. As it was, the two men could see little beyond the dim circles of light their flashlights cast – flashlights whose batteries should have been replaced days ago.

"Nah nah nah, she's expecting a big dinner for Valentine's Day. She'd like go down to Jameson's an' have the whole deal."

"So? Let her go. Damn women; always expect us men for pay. Hell, she want to go down? Well? You know where to tell her to go down," and Lalepa laughed at his own witticism.

"Hey, the only way *you* ever got a woman was by paying," his partner replied, and regretted his words as soon as he had said them.

Lalepa stopped and looked back through the darkness at the shorter wiry man.

"Oh, yeah? Is dat right? Well, in dat case even more reason for not lend you any my money. After all, gotta save so I can *pay* for one woman." And Lalepa started off again.

"Shit, I didn't mean it that way. Lalepa! Hey, Lalepa, come on. I just need a loan. I'll pay you back – honest."

"Honest? Geez! You? NO, las' time – NO! Now shut up about it."

Muttering under his breath Lalepa's partner shut up and concentrated on making his way over the rough floor of the lava tube. If they'd been in a section he was familiar with he would have picked up a rock and hurled it at Lalepa's back – and then run like hell. But they weren't in a familiar section of the lava tube network . . . and Lalepa would probably catch him and punch him good.

Since this was the first time the two men had been in this section of lava tubing they not only had to watch their footing but also pay attention to where they had been and where they were going. In the miles of lava tubes that make up the Kazumura Lava Field it was easy to get lost. Sometimes people who got lost here were found . . . other times their bones were found.

The two men had been on an assignment from their group. Having completed that assignment they headed out, but in order to keep their work secret they never entered and exited the lava tubes by the same route. Never having come this way before, and feeling a little lost, they were both beginning to get nervous. Neither one would mention that nervousness to the other however.

They would have turned back long ago except for the faint flow of air that came from behind them and indicated that there was an opening somewhere up ahead. An opening that they hoped would lead them out of the lava tube and into the daylight.

CHAPTER FIFTEEN

Lalepa thought about telling his partner to turn off his flashlight so that they could save its batteries. Lalepa knew it would be difficult having both of them guided only by his own flashlight. His partner might even trip and fall. Lalepa smiled at that. *Stupid horny asshole. Thinks with his dick all the time. Serve him right to mess up his face a little.*

With a grin Lalepa called back, "Hey, why not –"

Lalepa's suggestion was cut off when his partner stumbled and nearly fell through the wall on their right.

"Goddamn! What the hell?"

"What?" Lalepa barked.

His partner didn't answer immediately. Lalepa turned his flashlight back on him and was startled to see the other man halfway into the wall of the lava tube.

"Lalepa! Look! Look here!"

Lalepa stepped carefully over and peered through an opening in the wall of the lava tube. The crumbled lava rock at its base told him that the opening was recent. *Probably from either that last big earthquake, or one of the aftershocks.*

Together they shone their flashlights around the inside of the lava bubble that had been formed hundreds of years ago on the side of the tube. They could see on the right side of the bubble an older smaller tube filled with rubble that had probably been the original source of the bubble. Lava had forced its way in, formed the bubble, and then had flowed away before the lava inside the bubble could harden. Lapela guessed that over the years the roof of the small tube had collapsed leaving the bubble isolated.

Inside the lava bubble vague shapes intrigued the two men.

The slit that was the new opening into the bubble was barely wide enough for the men to enter, even when they sucked in their stomachs and turned sideways. But enter they did. Lalepa scraped and scratched himself getting in and thought, only for a moment, about the difficulty he would face should he have to get out of the bubble quickly. His partner slipped in easily, like a gecko hiding in a crack above a doorway . . . just waiting for an insect to make a mistake by getting too near.

"What the hell is this?" the wiry man asked.

"Shut up, bruddah. I don' know if we should be here."

The two men were familiar with gravesites. After all, they had just finished placing a bundle of ancient bones, wrapped in a beautiful kapa cloth, in a small niche high up on the wall of another section of lava tube much farther back. This had been their assignment for the day. Lapela had been selected earlier in the week from their group to carry out the reburial and had chosen the wiry man to accompany him. Very quietly, so as not to draw attention to themselves from anyone else exploring the lava tubes, they had chanted respectfully as they placed their bundle. A chant that they had memorized with great difficulty. Having finished their assignment Lalepa had chuckled to himself as they walked away. He enjoyed imagining the frustration on the face of the people at the museum when they asked for the bones back and were told that the hui, of which Lalepa and his partner were members, had "lost" the borrowed bones. Undoubtedly the museum would refuse to lend their group any more iwi or relics. Lalepa knew their hui would find another way to retrieve their ancestors' iwi and return them to their proper burial places.

But this was different. This was not a site any of the members of the hui had picked for reburial. This was an original burial site . . . a burial site of ancestors who were long gone from this world.

"Hey! Better we get da hell outta here," Lalepa pronounced, a slight tremor in his normally commanding voice. The hair on the back of his neck stood up as bumps like chickenskin rose on his arms.

His partner turned back from examining the relics in the cave with his flashlight.

"Why? What're you worried about? Jus' bones . . . same as we put back other times," but even as he remarked on the cave so casually the wiry man's heart beat ever more quickly. The bones that caused both men's hearts to beat faster appeared to be those of a man; an ancient kapa malo covering his hip bones confirmed this. A man who had chosen to die curled up on the floor of the chamber in front of a raised altar-like section at the back of the chamber. On top of this altar rested an ancient sennit casket known as a ka'ai. Besides the bones there were a number of other items which caused the wiry man's eyes to widen in wonder . . . and greed.

Lalepa saw the other items too, but his concern was more for the iwi. The accompanying items merely confirmed to him that this was the burial chamber of a high chief. Accompanying the chief in death were two canoe paddles of fine Koa wood, a one-person canoe with outrigger, three thin and very sharp wooden spears each about seven feet long, a large lei o mano club set all around with Tiger shark teeth, a feather helmet and a feather cape, a large calabash that had been cracked and mended perfectly on one side and, most frightening to Lalepa, the chief's god. The god looked to be a little over one foot tall, covered with tiny feathers plucked from island birds, with eyes formed from seashells and a fierce lopsided mouth lined with dogs teeth. His nose was flat and broad and the light from the flashlight beams made it appear as if he was staring at the two invaders of his home. Around the god's neck hung a lei niho pala'oa. The glistening white ivory carving appeared to be crafted from a whale's tooth while the hair supporting the carving was undoubtedly the chief's own hair. Lalepa knew from stories told him by his grandmother when he was a small boy that the mana, the power, of the chief was stored in that lei niho pala'oa and that the worst thing that could befall the chief while he was alive was for someone else to gain control of his lei niho pala'oa and thus of his mana.

Lalepa was so focused on the feathergod that he failed to notice the bundle off to the side. It had been placed carefully but was not accompanied with as many other items as the chief's bones were.

The wiry man noted the bundle. It was far less than six feet long and looked to be wrapped in silk, perhaps in a silk robe. He

43

shuddered a little as he guessed at what was wrapped in the silk. He could tell that the silk was good quality, even though it was covered in lava dust that had dropped down over the centuries. The colors of the silk, reds and greens and yellows, were still bright and vibrant, as much as they could be in the small amount of light in the chamber. At what the wiry man guessed must be the foot of the bundle, on a square of fine kapa cloth, lay an unbroken blue and white porcelain platter. Dark blue designs stood out against the white background of the plate. It was more concave than the platters the man was used to eating from, probably more of a soup or noodle dish. And probably worth quite a bit of money . . . but tough to carry out of the lava tube without breaking.

"Hey, Lalepa, you think maybe we take some of this stuff back with us? I might know a guy who'd be real happy to pay us for some of these things. "

"Shit, no! You crazy? We not take nothing from dis place! Come on, we get da hell out now."

"But Lalepa, look at all this stuff. I mean, well, we wouldn't touch the bones . . . but the rest of the stuff . . ."

"No! Belongs to him," and with a jerk of his head Lalepa indicated both the ka'ai with its bones and the feathered god. "You don't know about dis 'cuz you faddah never tell you. So trust me. We don' take nothing here."

The wiry man resented Lalepa's reference to his missing father. Yes, his father had cut out early in his young son's life, but that didn't give people the right to look down on him.

"C'mon, we go."

The wiry man followed along behind Lalepa, slowly. At the entrance to the bubble cave he paused and looked back at the items there with longing. Together Lalepa and the wiry man exited the burial cave, turned right, and continued following the breeze toward what they hoped was an opening up ahead. The breeze behind them grew stronger as if pushing them away from the burial cave.

"Look, Lalepa, light."

Lalepa grunted in affirmation and signaled that they should turn off their flashlights. The wiry man held his in his hand while Lalepa stuck his in the back pocket of his baggy shorts, its head protruding. The light ahead grew brighter and brighter until they were standing at the end of the lava tube . . . looking down at the froth of the sea as it hammered at the rocks some sixty feet below.

An idea began to form in the wiry man's mind.

Lalepa stood in the opening and looked down . . . then up . . . then off to either side. There was no way to climb out of the lava tube from here.

"We gotta go back," he pronounced and, turning, began to walk back into the lava tube tunnel.

His partner stepped up to the tunnel opening and looked down. Shading his eyes he peered at the rocks below and called back down the tunnel to Lalepa.

"Hey, I think I see a way. Yeah, it'll work. Come take a look."

Shaking his head in exasperation Lalepa retraced his steps until he stood beside his partner.

"Where?"

"There, see? Just to the right of that big boulder," said the wiry man as he stepped back so that Lalepa could see better.

"You nuts. No way we can go that way," Lalepa said looking up and then down. Straightening up he shook his head as he said, "Hell, break you neck try."

"Probably," said the wiry man as he struck Lalepa on the back of his head with his own flashlight. Even as he fell to his knees Lalepa's hands reached back to grasp his head where he had been struck. His partner wrenched the flashlight out of Lapela's back pocket, hit him again on the head with his own flashlight, and kicked the big man in the back as hard as he could. Like a massive Koa tree felled in the forest Lalepa keeled over and dropped out through the tunnel opening and down toward the rocks below. The wiry man jumped forward and was just in time to see Lalepa strike the big boulder below, bounce off to the left, strike another jagged outcropping of lava rock, and crash into the sea. Holding his breath the man waited and waited until finally he was rewarded with the sight of Lalepa's body floating face down in the waves. He watched for five minutes as the body was battered back and forth between the sharp rocks by the fierce waves. When he was sure Lalepa wasn't going to climb back up the face of the cliff to attack him the man stepped back from the opening.

Shaking his flashlight produced only the tinkling sounds of a broken bulb and other damaged parts. He drew back his hand to throw his flashlight into the ocean with Lalepa's body, then changed his mind and stuffed it into the left pocket of his shorts. Carrying Lalepa's flashlight in his right hand he headed back to the burial cave.

CHAPTER SIXTEEN

Back in the bubble cave the wiry man took visual inventory of the items there. Knowing that his flashlight wouldn't last forever and not wanting to exit the same way that Lalepa did he quickly made up his mind. Stripping off his tee shirt he laid it on the floor. Gently, so as not to damage it, he removed the lei niho pala`oa from around the neck of the feathered god. Careful not to touch the god itself he placed the lei in the large calabash, and then set the calabash on his tee shirt. He wrapped the shirt around the two articles he was taking, stood up, and used his flashlight to take one last look around the cave. Struck by the sight of the silk-wrapped bundle he stepped carefully over to that part of the cave, reached down carefully and slowly pulled back what turned out to indeed be a silk robe from the top of the bundle. He inhaled sharply at the sight that met his eyes. A man, actually more mummy than man, was wrapped in the silk robe. The man's black hair fastened into a long queue was still attached to his skull and lay draped over his chest. His eyes were long gone, but that didn't stop the empty sockets from staring out at the one who had disturbed his rest. The man noticed something else. He reached down and retrieved a knife, a common sailor's knife probably, that lay on the man's chest underneath his robe. It wasn't so very fancy but it caught his interest, and he always liked weapons. The man placed it in the calabash along with the lei niho pala`oa. He looked longingly again at the blue porcelain platter and decided that while he really wanted it, it was just too fragile to carry out of the cave. But the next time he came, and there would be a next time, he would bring something to carefully wrap it up in. He nodded his head in satisfaction at his future plans.

The thin man backed quickly away, slid through the opening in the lava tube wall, and scuttled down the tube and away from the light at the end.

On his way back to the surface, remembering the story of Hansel and Gretel that his mother had read to him as a child, he was careful to deposit pieces of Lalepa's broken flashlight at significant twists and turns in order to allow him to find his way back to the treasure cave.

CHAPTER SEVENTEEN
The Town of Kona
February 7, 2007

The sign on the window read –

ANTIQUES AND COLLECTIBLES

Specializing in Hawai`iana.

The shop itself was small and dark, crammed with numerous past treasures and memories that had been surrendered through necessity. Ideally located on Ali'i Drive it was only a short walk away from Hulihe'e Palace. Customers frequently found their way in after touring the palace. An old-fashioned bell over the door announced visitors as they entered. A much newer light blinked on the inside wall of the office toward the back of the shop whenever the front door opened. An even newer monitor and recorder sat on the desk of that office linked to a tiny camera mounted high on the wall and aimed at the same front door in order to record the comings and goings of all who entered the shop.

Sherman Richards stood behind a massive free-form koa wood desk. Like the desk he was a massive man, though primarily massive from side to side. Also like the desk he was shiny on top – and somewhat slippery. The smile on his face never quite reached his eyes; eyes which could tell the worth of an antique, or the amount of money in a buyers' pocket, to the dime. The desk bore a discreet price tag, *$9,000* written in elegant script on a small embossed card taped to the top of the desk. Pulling open a drawer in the desk Richards extracted a piece of red velvet eighteen inches square. He laid the velvet out on the desktop then reached behind the desk and brought up a grey stone poi pounder. Placing the poi pounder in the center of the red velvet Richards turned to the man beside him.

"Just as I promised," Richards said flashing his teeth in a smile. "I can absolutely guarantee that this poi pounder is over three hundred years old. It belonged to a family whose ancestors lived in this very area at the time that Captain Cook discovered these islands. They only agreed to part with it because of – financial difficulties."

Richards did not elaborate on the financial difficulties, which involved the sudden death of the husband and the need of his wife to bury him properly. He also did not think it necessary to mention that he had paid only two hundred dollars for the three-century-old relic.

"And how much do you want for this item, Mr. Richards?" the customer asked.

"For you? You have been such a good customer . . . and you have such excellent taste. Why I believe that by now your *private* collection of Hawai`iana exceeds my own."

"You flatter me . . . as usual. How much?"

Richards let out his breath in a show of indecision and rubbed the bald spot on top of his head.

"One thousand five hundred . . . and I make very little on this transaction," he was quick to add.

A soft melody played a brief tune in the back office.

"Excuse me, let me just see who is calling," Richards said as he set off the maze created by the plethora of items for sale.

"I'll only be a moment," he called back to his customer as he stepped into the small office and closed the glass-paneled door behind him. With the door closed he was able to talk freely on the phone while still observing the interior of his shop through the large glass window set into the office wall.

"Yes? Really? Are you sure? And just when do you think you might . . .? Ah, I see. Certainly, I may be interested. Get back to me . . . and remember, discreetly."

After replacing the wireless phone in its cradle James stood for a moment, his eyes seeing something beyond the confines of his shop. With a shake of his shoulders he returned to the present. Opening the office door and stepping out he returned to his customer who was holding the ancient stone poi pounder and turning it upside down in order to better examine its base.

"You know, it really deserves to be in a private collection such as yours, not just on display for *tourists* to gloss over. Of course, I thought of you first . . . but I do have other clients . . ."

The customer hefted the poi pounder again, returned it to the red velvet cloth and, making up his mind, nodded in agreement.

"Have it delivered. By Friday afternoon. I'm giving a party."

"Certainly," Richards responded.

He picked up the poi pounder and prepared to carry it back to his office. He paused and turned back again. Still cradling the stone relic in his arms he smiled once more at his customer.

"I should let you know that, uh, I may soon have something quite nice coming into my shop. Something that I believe you will be most interested in. Something of quite a collectible nature. Of course, you must realize that something of the quality I'm talking about comes with a much more substantial price tag."

Richards inclined his head slightly to his customer, who responded with a brief nod and a thin smile. Richards slipped back into his office to put the stone relic aside for packaging and mailing, while his customer continued to quietly prowl the store.

CHAPTER EIGHTEEN
Saturday, February 10, 2007

Son of a bitch! Why does she have to live up here? The wiry man was not enjoying his early-morning drive. Early-morning was not his favorite time of day since he worked mostly afternoons and evenings at his regular job. A one-lane dirt road, heavily rutted, climbing up the mountain wasn't what he was used to driving. He wondered for the tenth time since leaving his place whether or not he should just use a couple of old towels. *Got plenty beach towels from the hotel.*

Swinging around a sharp left turn in the road he got over too far on the shoulder and nearly took out a banana tree. Actually it nearly took him out. The maneuver almost made him lose the cigarette dangling from his lip. Cursing some more he swung back into the middle of the road. *This is a road? Shit, I've followed better pig trails.*

A right turn now and he saw a whitewashed post marking a break in the greenery to his left. He swung down this even narrower path, the shrubbery on either side whacking at him through his open window. Two hundred yards further in and the path he was following opened out into a freshly-mown circle of natural grass. This formed a lawn a full thirty yards in diameter. At the back of the circle sat a pleasant little house, painted even brighter white than the marking post back on the road. A lanai ran across the front, down the two sides and undoubtedly across the back, circling the whole house. Off to the right side of the house stood a tiny pre-fab metal garage. The garage's open door revealed a 2006 Jeep Wrangler four-wheel drive painted bright red. Squeezed in beside the Wrangler was a very old, very rusted dirt bike. Everything about it looked worn, except the engine. The engine sparkled.

The wiry man parked off to the left side of the mown circle in the shade given by several large Pandanus trees. Two of them evidently had recently made contributions of their leaves.

He took one more deep drag on his cigarette before dropping it on the ground. He took one step before turning around to grind the butt out. No point starting off on the wrong foot . . . if he could help it.

He walked up the four steps to the house, but stopped before stepping onto the lanai itself. Rapping loudly on the support post he called out, "Grace! Hey, Gracie? You here?" If his luck was bad she could be out in the fields tending her coffee trees. Then he'd either have to wait, maybe most of the day, or he'd have to give up and go back to Kona and try again . . . when?

Luck was with him today.

"I'm in here. Take off your slippahs."

Leaving his slippers outside by the door, he cracked open the screen door and slipped into the house. Darker and cooler inside. He waited for his eyes to adjust here in the main room of the house. Part living room, part workshop. The smell of coffee beans competed with other smells – those of lauhala and various dyes

Along the walls new and old chests crouched. Two sideboards of indeterminate age groaned under the weight of stacks of magazines and dried gourds filled with scrapers. Kapa beaters and other tools lay where they had last been set down after being used. Through one door he could see a kitchen with a polished wood plank floor. An old Formica table, sagging in the middle, stood in the center of the kitchen. Through a door at the opposite end of the room he could just make out a bed covered with a red and white Hawai`ian quilt. In one corner of the main room stood tall baskets overflowing with Pandanus leaves already dried and bleached and just waiting to be scraped. On the walls hooks supported hats and fans and purses. A fabric-covered couch along one wall was buried under large decorated pieces of kapa, pieces waiting to be bought by tourists and hung up on walls back home in Indiana or Iowa. Or maybe just put away in a closet to be dragged out now and then as thoughts drifted back to that long-ago trip to the islands. Lauhala mats covered the floor almost completely and provided a comfortable working space for the lone occupant of the room.

Sitting in the middle of the room, patiently painting the last bits of an intricate geometric design onto a remarkably thin piece of kapa a thin light-brown woman with hard eyes squinted up at the wiry man. She put her brush down resting it on the edge of a small bowl. She picked up the beer bottle beside the bowl and took a long drink.

"So?"

"Ahh, my beautiful wahine. You are timeless."

"Screw you, you conniving buggah."

"Aww, Gracie – "

"Don't *Aww, Gracie*, me. The only time I see you is when you need something. So, what you want? Gotta be pretty important for you drive out here. You need coffee? Got plenty this year. Good crop. I'll give you a good price if you haul it yourself."

The wiry man walked over the soft mats toward the woman and squatted down on his heels beside the piece of kapa she was working on.

"This is really nice. Should make you a lot of dough."

Gracie tilted her head to one side looking at him. She took another sip of beer.

"Maybe," she said. "You looking for kapa?"

"You're the best artist around," he said not answering her directly, but rather trying to appeal to her ego.

"One of the best," she replied, flattered despite her caution.

"No, the best. That's why I beat myself ragged on that pig path you call a road out there."

Gracie laughed, "You try that on a bike sometime. Your skinny okole would be black and blue."

They chuckled a bit at that image, both admitting the truth of it.

"Okay," Gracie repeated, "what you want?"

"I need three pieces, one big, two not-so-big."

"For what?"

"A deal."

Gracie nodded her head. "A deal. One of your deals? Cash
. . . upfront."

"Of course, Gracie, of course."

Gracie levered herself up from her sitting position and
stretched her back. The wiry man rose also and stood waiting for her,
his hand at his side. The fingers of his hand beat rapidly on his thigh.

"Here, come look these."

Gracie led him over to a large old coffee table in front of the
couch. Stacks of fine kapa separated by size filled the table. Gracie
cleared a space and they sat down on the couch. Gracie proceeded to
show the wiry man various pieces in different colors. She managed to
get him to tell her that he wanted to wrap several *pieces of Hawai`iana*
that he had for sale in kapa so that they would show better. Gracie
guessed that his *pieces of Hawai`iana* were either stolen or fake, but
she kept her thoughts to herself.

After selecting three pieces of fairly nice kapa they debated the
price for a while. Eventually Gracie collected twenty dollars each for
the two small pieces and thirty-five dollars for the larger piece. She
wrapped the three pieces individually in old newspaper.

Tucking his purchases under his arm the wiry man made ready
to leave. Just before he got to the door he noticed a small boulder
sitting on the floor beside the screen door. Two petroglyphs were
carved into the boulder.

"Nice, where you get?"

"Jackson give me that. Pretty good, eh? Can not tell from the
original."

"Very nice. Jackson No'eau? I think I know him. Works
down at the park in Kona on the weekends? Does petroglyph
drawings to sell to the tourists?"

"That's him."

"Good work," the wiry man said, even as he thought about the
money he might be able to make selling *Original Petroglyphs* to a few
dealers he knew. It was something to think about for the future.

"A hui hou, Gracie."

Gracie just gave him a casual wave. She had closed the door and gone back to her work before he had started his engine.

With the three pieces of kapa on the seat beside him he silently cursed Gracie and her sharp dealing. He'd spent twenty-five dollars more than he'd planned on. He hoped that the kapa wrapping would help get him top dollar when he met with his dealer tomorrow.

He lit a cigarette and tossed the still-burning match out the window. Fortunately for Gracie the match landed on a bare piece of ground and burned out innocently. As he pulled out of Gracie's driveway and back down the dirt road one angry thought rode with him. *What a bitch! She didn't even offer me a beer!*

CHAPTER NINETEEN
Early Morning, Sunday
February 11, 2007

The light blinked back in the office but, amazingly, the bell over the door didn't ring. If he checked the videotape Sherman Richards guessed he would probably find that the wiry local man walking through the store toward him had reached up just as he cracked open the door and had placed his fingers between the striker and the bell.

Sherman shrugged. He regarded the man as something akin to a reptile, but a useful reptile. One that he had trained.

"Hey, howzit, Mr. Richards?"

Richards' reply was simply a look of distaste, which served to mask the greed behind his eyes.

"What do you have for me this time?"

The man's smile broadened showing teeth heavily stained with nicotine . . . and a few of them missing.

"First class items! All of them. And you know I bring them to you first. Always."

"You bring them to me because I give you the best price, and because taking them anywhere else might land you in jail," Richards said ominously. He was pleased at the glint of fear in his supplier's eyes. "Here, put them down on this desk," Richards said indicating the same koa wood desk he had used when displaying the poi pounder.

The brown-skinned man swung a backpack off his shoulders and took satisfaction in the slight wince Richards gave when it thumped onto the desk. Opening the pack he extracted three packages, each wrapped in soft fine-woven new kapa cloth.

Richards' supplier unwrapped the middle package first and displayed the lei niho pala`oa. The man heard Richards suck in his breath and knew that he had brought in a valuable piece of merchandise.

"So?" he asked quietly.

Richards endeavored to tear his gaze away from the beautifully carved piece in front of him.

"What else do you have?" he said, with just a touch of anticipation.

The man unwrapped the second package to reveal a very old calabash, cracked and expertly repaired on one side. Richards wet his lips. With a wave of his hand he indicated the third and smallest package.

When this package was opened Richards was disappointed to see that it held only an old knife with a carved handle in the shape of a Chinese dragon. Yet he was also pleased because it gave him an edge in negotiating for all three of the items. He saw that the knife was old, and probably Chinese, but it was also plain and had seen quite a bit of use.

"You disappoint me," Richards said crossing his arms over his chest.

"What? Terrific stuff here. You see this?" and the supplier picked up the lei niho pala`oa by the knot of hair and swung it back and forth. It was all Richards could do to keep from snatching it out of the man's hand and placing it gently back down on the kapa.

"Yes, granted that item is not too worn . . . But the knife shows a great deal of abuse. And the calabash . . . well it's nice but it also is very common. Was there nothing else with these . . . items?"

The supplier felt his prices being whittled away and looked for a way to shore them up.

"Sure, but no can go back dat place for a while. Got to let it cool a bit. Das why I bring you da best of what I find. You know well as me, all dis belong one chief!" and he thrust the lei niho pala`oa toward Richards' face. "Now, how much for everything?"

The supplier and Richards both knew that the advantage lay in getting the other man to name a price first.

"Everything? Who says I want everything? I'm overstocked now in this store. I've got to move some of my current merchandise before I can even think about bringing in new items. And some of my best clients have begun looking more and more over on Maui for their purchases. I just don't know whether or not I can even afford any of these items . . ."

The supplier panicked thinking that maybe Richards might not buy any of his new merchandise. He also knew that Richards was really his only buyer on the island, the only one that he could bring this sort of merchandise to anyway.

"Hey, this all," he swept his arm over the desk, "worth at least two thousand dollar."

Richards had him. He brought his hand up to his chin and rubbed it as if deep in thought.

Reluctantly he said, "Ahh, maybe . . . maybe six hundred."

"Six hundred! Shit I better off put 'em back in da cave."

And thus they entered into their final round of negotiations for the day.

* * *

As his supplier walked out the door, this time letting the bell jingle behind him, Richards closed and locked the door. Returning to the desk he looked down on his new acquisitions for a few moments. Retrieving two blank cards along with a black marking pen from the desk drawer, he wrote out prices on each card before affixing them to the new merchandise he had for sale. The sailor's knife, labeled *Antique Chinese Sailor's Knife $300,* went in the front window next to a walking stick and a cut-glass vase. The calabash found a place on an old buffet that had been shipped out from New England many years ago. Its' label read *Authentic Hawai`ian Calabash $950.* He thought to himself that he would need to use some furniture polish on the calabash to really make it shine. The kapa cloth pieces that had wrapped each of the items he folded neatly and put away in another desk drawer. They might be useful when he sold some of the smaller items in his store. In any event, it had been pleasurable to force his supplier to include them with the three items he had bought.

Next Richards carefully wrapped the lei niho pala`oa in a piece of red silk cloth.  He tied the new bundle up with a bright yellow ribbon and, proceeding to his office in the back of the shop, carefully locked it in a large safe there.  He put no price tag on the lei niho pala`oa, but in his mind various sums danced about . . . all large five-figure amounts.

* * *

Richards' supplier walked down the street toward the parking lot where he had left his aging pickup truck. He hoped that the old parking permit on the dash, carefully folded to hide most of the printed date so that the parking attendant might think it was current, had kept him from getting a ticket. *Greedy buggahs! Even charge fo' parking Sundays.*

He surreptitiously patted his front pocket to assure himself that the money Richards had paid him was still there. One thousand and fifty dollars. Dang, he'd really sweated the money out of Richards this time.

CHAPTER TWENTY
Friday, May 11, 2007
Palo Alto, California

Felica was feeling mixed emotions. On the one hand it was a lovely Spring day with abundant sunshine and soft breezes here on the campus of Stanford University. On the other hand she would much rather be back in the City taking her time while getting ready to go out to dinner with her boyfriend Jeremy Pono. Then again she had been able to find a parking space close to Encina Hall here on campus; close to her cramped little office in the Department of Cultural and Social Anthropology where she worked as a Research Assistant while pursuing her Doctoral degree.

But parking spaces were much easier to come by on Fridays – and she generally did not come in to her office on Friday. However she was happy to do so whenever Professor Simon Thompson, her boss and also her Doctoral program advisor, needed her. After all, he had been instrumental in getting Felicia her position as his lecture assistant and paper reader/grader, though she didn't really like also functioning as his *go-fer*. Well, whatever it was had better be important enough that it couldn't wait until Monday. Felicia's heels clicked on the pavement, echoing her impatience. *Okay let's see what this is all about*, she thought as she pushed through the doors to Encina Hall, strode over to the elevator and pressed the UP button.

Two minutes later Felicia knocked perfunctorily before opening the door and entering Professor Thompson's office. The office seemed much smaller than it actually was, due largely to the fact that every wall was given over to floor-to-ceiling bookshelves, and these bookshelves were crowded to overflowing not only with books but also with artifacts collected by Professor Thompson in his many years of study and exploration throughout the world. He called them his *prizes*, as if he had won them. They included a blowgun from somewhere along the Amazon River, a baby's sarcophagus from a remote tomb in Egypt and the lower jaw, complete with tusks, of a hippopotamus. On one shelf there was a highly polished box, rosewood Felicia thought, that contained the Professor's most precious treasure. Once when Felicia entered the Professor's office without knocking she had surprised him with the box open on his desk as he held the contents of the box in his hands, turning it this way and that way as he examined it. Upon asking Felicia learned that this was a mokomokai from New Zealand. Never having seen one before Felicia had been forced to ask the Professor to explain the grotesque object.

"It's a shrunken head basically, but with ritualistic tattoos covering the face. I don't know the full story behind this particular one, but many were slaves who were forcibly tattooed just so they could be killed, decapitated and their heads shrunk in order to be traded to the English for guns. With which the Maori then killed more of their rivals, took their heads to shrink and trade for more guns. Quite a brutal practice."

Over the past eighteen months Felicia had seen and handled most of the artifacts and many of the books, so it was easier for her to ignore them and focus her attention on the two men in the room.

Professor Thompson sat behind his desk smoking a large curved pipe in direct contravention of University rules. A quiet fan on the edge of his desk blew most of the smoke out the half-open window behind him. Across from him with his back to Felicia sat another man who Felicia knew well, though she avoided him as much as possible.

"Ah, Felicia, please take a seat," Professor Thompson said as he indicated the other chair facing his desk.

Felicia sat down, shifting her chair slightly farther away from the man in the other chair. Felicia sat with her knees pointed up, a result of the fact that both the chair she was in and the chair the other man occupied had much shorter legs than normal. Consequently all visitors to the Professor's office sat looking up at him. Felicia turned slightly in her chair to face the other man.

"Hwang Tam."

"Felicia. How . . . good . . . to see you today," Hwang Tam replied in English touched with a slight British accent that revealed his educational background. His smile was forced.

"And you too," Felicia replied with her own smile looking like it might crack her face.

They both turned back to Professor Thompson who took his pipe out of his mouth and balanced it in the top of his empty coffee cup.

"Well, pleasantries aside I asked you both to come in because we have been asked to undertake a small bit of work for the University." Professor Thompson leaned back in his chair and folded his hands over his stomach.

"Oh, please, not another outhouse excavation!" Felica exclaimed.

Professor Thompson chuckled a bit before leaning forward onto his desk again.

"Felicia? You mean you didn't enjoy our small dig last month in Nevada City?"

Felica opened her mouth to reply, let the air out of her lungs, took another breath and spoke more calmly.

"I certainly appreciate all that we learned, Professor. But it just still amazes me how the stench of an outdoor privy can permeate the soil even after a hundred years. Granted, we found some very meaningful artifacts . . . still, I would prefer not to repeat that type of dig for quite a while."

"It must have been particularly noxious for someone of your . . . delicate breeding," Hwang Tam said in an overly solicitous tone.

"Someone of my *delicate* breeding?"

Felicia started to turn her chair to face Hwang Tam, who, in his turn leaned his right elbow on the arm of his chair while keeping his hand tucked in his jacket pocket. He gave Felicia a smug smile.

Felicia opened and closed her mouth twice, crossed her arms across her chest and smiled back at Hwang.

"You know, Hwang, I never did thank you for giving me a . . . hand during that dig."

The blood rushed to Hwang Tam's face but Professor Thompson spoke up before either Hwang Tam or Felicia could carry their verbal battle any further.

"That will be enough. We have other matters before us," and picking up a computer printout page Professor Thompson put on his reading glasses, adjusted them to his satisfaction and began to speak in his best lecture mode.

"There's been a find on the Big Island of Hawai`i. A hotel there is adding some tennis courts down by a beach. It's along a very nice bay, I understand. They began excavations and almost immediately started turning up bones. They're fairly certain that these are native bones, but, as is usual in these cases over there, they would like some authentication by archeologists."

Felicia and Hwang Tam both made to speak but Professor Thompson held up his hand and continued reading.

"You both probably were going to ask why they didn't ask someone nearer to them. Well, there are some other sites being examined right now by local archeologists and the hotel wants to proceed as quickly as possible, can't wait for the local folks to finish up with the other sites. Also, there's some local native group that has had bad experiences with some of the local archeologists over the past few years. They're pushing for some outsiders, us, to come in with a fresh, probably meaning more receptive to their views, outlook."

Professor Thompson put the printout back on his desk, steepled his hands and looked over the top of his reading glasses at his two assistants.

"I thought maybe the two of you might enjoy a little vacation, paid for by this hotel and endorsed by the University. Hwang Tam . . . your study year here is almost over. A chance to visit Hawai`i before returning to Beijing University . . . should look pretty good to you. Felicia, I believe you have family on the Big Island?"

"Actually, Professor, my fiancé's family lives there. My family is in San Francisco."

"Even better, give you a chance to see if you'll fit into his family . . . you know, meet your mother-in-law . . . while you still have time to back out of the wedding."

Felicia shook her head slightly while biting her lower lip.

"But Professor," Hwang Tam interrupted, "I still have a few more leads here at the University that I would like to follow up on."

"In regard to your . . . theory, I imagine."

Professor Thompson's forehead wrinkled slightly as he shook his head.

"I would think that all the paths you've tried to trace over this past year, all those dead-ends would have convinced you that your theory, while quite interesting, is not verifiable."

Hwang Tam sat up straighter in his chair.

"On the contrary, Professor. I remain convinced of the soundness of my theory. I am sure that China was pre-eminent in exploration of the New World."

"You are sure, but you have no proof, nothing irrefutable."

"I thought surely that the anchor . . ."

"Yes, it is definitely an anchor off a Chinese treasure ship. But finding it in the Sacramento River does not prove that it came off a treasure ship. With all the Chinese settlements along the Sacramento it was more likely brought over by some fisherman who obtained it . . . well, who knows where."

"But the logbook . . ."

"I've examined the logbook as you asked me to. While it is very interesting, there is nothing in that logbook to prove conclusively that the treasure ship it came from reached this shore. And as for your idea that the treasure ship also reached Hawai`i, well all I will say there is that it is obvious that the ship touched some Polynesian islands, but those islands could well have been located nearer Fiji and the Marquessas than Hawai`i."

Hwang Tam opened his mouth to rebut the Professor, but Professor Thompson cut him off.

"No, I'm sorry Hwang Tam. You've had a year to do research here at Stanford. You've had access to our library and to our archives. You've examined all the relevant relics that we have here. You have proven nothing. However, your assistance in our endeavors has been appreciated." Professor Thompson picked up his pipe, lit it on the second match and leaned back again in his chair.

"Now, back to our examination of the newly-discovered bones on the Big Island. I've told the hotel, and the University, that we will arrive there on Tuesday, May twenty-second. The University will arrange for our flight over. The hotel, by the way, is the Queen's Beach Resort Hotel. It's a good way up the Kohala coast and I hear it is very nice. We will need to contact the hotel to see if they can accommodate us. Otherwise we will have to stay in Kona and I understand that the drive up to the hotel is not a short one."

"Professor?"

"Yes, Felicia?"

"I believe I can help with that. One of my fiancé's sisters is the general manager of the Queen's Beach Resort Hotel. If you'd like I could call her and see about rooms for the three of us."

"Very good! See what you can do about that. Now, if there's nothing more? Then we leave on the twenty-second. Should only take us a couple of days to come to some conclusion about the bones these people over there have found. We may even have extra time to soak up some Hawaiian sun, and mai tais, before we have to return."

* * *

Immediately upon leaving the Professor's office Felicia called Jeremy on her cell phone and together they arranged to meet later that afternoon. But before they met, Felicia dropped by her hair salon and got her stylist to fit her in for a haircut.

As she watched her long blond hair falling to the floor Felicia thought to herself, *Well, with the humidity over in the islands short hair will probably be a lot more convenient.*

CHAPTER TWENTY-ONE
Saturday, May 12, 2007

Felicia rolled over slowly and quietly until she could look at Jeremy, covered partly by a bedsheet, sleeping beside her. She liked looking at him as he slept. His dark black hair was disarranged, but in a way that she found charming. His smooth chest, shoulders and arms didn't bulge with muscles, but they did reflect strength. Felicia reached out and gently placed her hand on his chest. He didn't wake up. She watched as her hand rode his chest with his regular breathing. She was fascinated once more at the contrast of his evenly colored brown skin with her own pale white skin. *Shark bait*, that was what Jeremy had called her when they first met. He had been right. He had been the shark, and she had been the bait that caught him. Their first lovemaking had been as frantic and urgent as a shark's feeding frenzy. Felicia loved being with Jeremy, loved going out with him, loved taking him to meet her friends.

Her mother had been less than pleased to meet Jeremy. She had made that face, the face that seemed to indicate that she was being forced to interact with something unpleasant . . . but that for civility's sake she was going to put up with that unpleasant something. Felicia enjoyed forcing her mother to interact with Jeremy almost as much as she enjoyed reminding her mother that she had chosen to study Archeology rather than something more . . . acceptable. Not that her mother was intimately involved with Felicia's upbringing. No, that responsibility had fallen on her nanny. After all, her mother had so many other activities to occupy her time. Belonging to some twenty plus organizations and groups did tend to demand a lot from you. It was only natural that other things had to take a backseat.

From thoughts of her mother Felicia branched out to thoughts of Jeremy's mother. She barely knew the woman, having met her only a few times over the course of two days while she accompanied

Jeremy to the funeral of his sister's husband, Frank. *One strong woman. Eyes that bore right into you. Protective of her children . . . especially Jeremy I bet. I wonder what her history is. Dark like Jeremy, but handsome too. If we had children I wonder . . .* She pushed that thought away. Children were a far-off goal for Felicia. Not a part of the here and now. She glanced at the bedside table with several condom packages strewn across it . . . two of them had been opened. As long as they were careful the thought of children, along with their actuality, could remain far in the future.

Leaning in closer Felicia breathed deep of the musky scent of Jeremy . . . Jeremy after lovemaking. It was a raw scent that always made her heart beat faster. Removing her hand from his chest she slid the bedsheet down as far as she could reach. He still didn't wake so she contented herself with just running her eyes over his body again.

Soon she was less than content with just running her eyes over his body. Jeremy awoke to her caresses, stretched, smiled broadly and took her gently into his arms.

* * *

Afterwards they lay spent in a tangle of arms and legs and bedsheet.

"That was an excellent idea," Jeremy said.

Barely awake and trying to push aside a growing need to pee Felicia responded, "What idea?"

"To come back to your place after dinner last night. I really didn't want to listen to the Symphony down at the Opera House." He leaned in to kiss her on the forehead, "This was so much more enjoyable." He ran his hand through her now short blond hair, "Though *this* is going to take some getting used to – but that doesn't mean I don't like it."

"Glad you liked both," and no longer able to resist the urge Felicia flung off the bedsheet and raced to the bathroom. She left the door slightly ajar so she could talk with Jeremy.

"I think I should call your sister at the hotel . . . Lori?"

"Yeah, she's the number three daughter. What for?"

"The project that the University assigned us. Remember, the dig at the hotel? Bones? Native relics?"

"Oh yeah, yeah . . . yeah, I remember now."

"What time is it over there?"

Jeremy retrieved his watch from the bedside table. Then, noticing the debris on the floor, he picked up the three used condoms with a tissue, balled them up and tossed them into a nearby wastepaper basket. He didn't notice that one of the three was split.

Rubbing his eyes to clear the sleep from them, he squinted at his watch. *Damn, I can't need glasses*, he thought.

"Almost noon here, so only nine in the morning there."

"Too early to call," Felicia said coming out of the bathroom and flopping down on the bed. Jeremy silently wished she hadn't jostled him. His bladder was just as full as hers had been.

"Probably. Why don't we take a drive, go down the coast. How about down to Pillar Point? We could get something to eat, have a late lunch, check out the harbor. How does that sound? You can call when we get back."

"It sounds good, very good. I need to shower first though – I smell."

Coming out from under the bedsheet Jeremy pinned Felicia down with his body.

"You smell wonderful. But I need to pee before you shower," he said rolling off her and sprinting for the bathroom.

"Lift the seat!" Felicia shouted at the closing door.

CHAPTER TWENTY-TWO
General Manager's Office
Queen's Beach Resort Hotel

Teri Maegher, her mother Haunani Pono and Haunani's daughter Lori Pono sat at the six-foot long oval highly-polished conference table in Lori's General Manager's office. The mugs of hot tea that Lori's assistant had brought them rested on circles of koa wood backed with thick cork. Teri and Haunani looked over one copy of a list placed on the table so they both could see it. Lori held her copy of the same list up a little closer to her face.

"Why don't you wear your glasses?" Haunani asked.

"I don't like the frames."

"Then buy new frames."

"You don't understand, Mom."

"Sure I do. You're getting vain. You think your glasses make you look older and with all these rich buggahs you have to keep happy you're afraid old will equate with incompetent."

Haunani struck closer to home than she knew. But Lori was not going to admit it.

"Can we get back to the guest list?"

"It looks like a pretty full luau," Teri commented.

Haunani let out an exasperated breath before returning her attention to the guest list.

"One hundred and twelve. Eighty-seven from the hotel alone. Going to be a busy night."

"Yeah, I can just hear Shari whining now about how much her feet are going to hurt her the next day. You know, they wouldn't hurt so much if she'd wear some sensible shoes instead of those four-inch heels. One of these days she's going to take a tumble walking the paths and then . . . "

"I know, I know," Haunani waved her hand in the air dismissing that topic. "So, any problems we need to work on?"

Both of the other women thought and then shook their heads.

"Good, so now we can . . ."

A soft knock preceded the opening of the door to Lori's office.

"Sorry to interrupt, Lori, but there's a phone call for you."

"Can't they wait?"

"Probably, but I thought since your mom and sister were both here you might want to take it. It's your brother's fiancé calling from California."

* * *

"Aloha, Felicia. How are things going over there? Tell Jeremy that if he doesn't treat you right his sisters are going to come over and pound on him – just like we did when he was a little keiki over here."

Teri leaned in toward the phone, "Hey, Felicia, remind him that as the caboose in this family he's got very little pull."

Haunani sat there shaking her head at her two daughter's shameful behavior. And chuckling to herself.

"Yeah? Really? Wow, that's great! No, I didn't request you special. I'm just really happy that they picked you. How many? When? Oh, shoot . . . that just might be a problem."

"What is it?" Teri asked.

"What's the problem?" Haunani added.

"Just a minute," Lori said into the phone before covering the mouthpiece.

"Good and bad news. You know we found lots of iwi when we started digging for the new tennis court down toward the beach?" Both of the other women nodded. "Well, the hotel is bound by the SMA," when her mother and sister looked blankly at her Lori explained, "the Shoreline Management Agreement. It's binding on us. When we find bones on our property we have to stop work immediately and investigate to see if it can be verified as an Hawaiian burial ground. If it is – well, we have to follow certain protocol in digging up and reburying the bones. Including a blessing ceremony to accompany the reburial."

"So? How is that a problem?" said Teri while Haunani just nodded in understanding of the issues involved.

"Felicia has been picked as one of the archeologists to come over here to the hotel and investigate the burial site. She, along with her boss, Professor Thompson, and some exchange-type student from China, Hwang something, are all supposed to arrive on the island on Monday, May twenty-second."

"As I said, what's the problem?"

Lori took her hand off the mouthpiece.

"Felicia? Yeah, hang in there I'll be right back with you."

Lori replaced her hand on the mouthpiece and continued her explanation to Teri and Haunani.

"I don't have any rooms for them. We've got a conference of doctors coming in on the Saturday before. They'll be here for the whole week and we're booked solid, one hundred percent! I have absolutely no place to put them. I couldn't even cram the three of them into one room . . . even if they'd put up with that. And yet I need to have them here. The local sovereignty group, Malama Pono, has protested us using any archeologists from the islands. They claim that those people have a bias that negatively impacts the re-burial process. The judge down in Kona that they took their protest to agreed with them and said that we, the hotel, should find someone from off-island to do the investigation. I left it up to our legal department, and Todd Miyamoto, he's the head of the department, approached Stanford University. Todd got his B.A there. Stanford said yes. And now I'm stuck between a rock and hard place."

Lori ran her fingers through her dark black hair; bottle-black Shari claimed, and Lori didn't protest too much at Shari's claims. Teri thought that she could see some white roots in Lori's hair, especially since she had recently had a short summer-cut. Somewhat too short Teri thought.

"No problem."

Lori and Teri turned their attention to Haunani.

"No?" "Why not?"

"We have plenty of room up at the hale. Two men? They can share a room. Felicia? Well, I could share my room with her . . . "

"No, Mom, it'd be easier for me to share my . . . " Teri's response came just slightly before her realization that her mother had maneuvered her again, just as she had so many times before.

Haunani smiled as Teri grimaced at being played so easily.

"I guess you're right, Teri," Haunani said innocently.

"Yeah, Mom," Teri responded ruefully.

"Is that okay then?" Lori asked the two women.

When they both nodded *yes* Lori returned to Felicia on the phone.

"Felicia? No problem. We worked it out. Haunani says that the three of you can stay up at the Pono Family Hale. It's nice up there, great views of the ocean and less than fifteen minutes down to the hotel. Are you going to have a rental car? No? Okay. Well, look, why don't you send me all your flight information. You have my email don't you? Okay then. We'll arrange for someone to meet the three of you and guide you up to the house. Any special requirements? No? Okay then, I'll wait for your email. Right. Right. Aloha."

Lori turned back to Teri and Haunani with a large weight lifted from her back.

"Thank you, that helps a great deal."

"As I said, no problem. Besides," Haunani went on, "this will give us a chance to check on this girl that Jeremy seems to have picked for his wife."

"We just saw her back in April at the funeral," Lori said, then, realizing her mistake, wished desperately to have her words back.

Teri looked down at her lap, a tear forming in the corner of her right eye.

Haunani reached over and put her hand on Teri's shoulder and let it rest there a moment before speaking.

"Yes, but Frank's funeral didn't really allow us time to get to know her very well. I was pleased that Jeremy came, and even more pleased that Felicia came with him and honored Frank's memory with her presence. But that time was devoted to Frank, and to Teri, and was too sad a time to get to know what Felicia is truly like. Remember, they were only able to stay for two days. One day before the funeral with the visit to the mortuary, and one day for the funeral itself. They flew back to Honolulu so early the next morning that we didn't even get to say goodbye to them at the airport. This trip over will give us a chance to see what sort of an addition Felicia might make to our ohana. After all, it's my duty as a mother to make sure that any daughter-in-law is suitable for my son."

Teri gave a short laugh at her mother's concern for Jeremy, looked away from the other women so that she could sweep the tear from her eye without either of them seeing, blinked twice and sat up straighter.

"Which room shall we put the two men in?"

"I was thinking that we could give them the front room off of the living room."

Teri's eyes widened a little at that thought.

"But there's still some of Frank's things in there."

"I know, but you have everything of yours moved out and into the back bedroom, next to my room. And the only things of Frank's that are still in that room are things like his golf clubs and a few of his tools."

Teri realized that Haunani was right. She had Frank's wedding ring, and their photo albums, his watch, some postcards and other items that they'd collected together over the years. She'd given away all his clothes, to a homeless shelter down in Kona. Except for his shirt. The shirt he had been wearing when he died. The shirt with his scent still on it . . . and his blood soaked into it. His shirt that every morning Teri still retrieved from the closet in the bedroom that had been theirs and held to her, and pressed her face into. Just to have one more faint scent of her husband. In that same closet, his golf clubs. She didn't know why she hadn't given those away yet. Maybe after

74

Felicia and her colleagues were gone. The clubs could sit in the closet in that bedroom for now. *Maybe Sean will take up golf. Maybe I should keep them for him.*

Teri still remembered the funeral services for Frank. She had desperately wanted Sean to be there, but had to content herself with flying over to California after Frank's funeral in order to attend the very small, very private wedding ceremony that Sean and Meagan had decided on. Teri had been delighted to see the two of them marry. Meagan's mother had been less than delighted – first because of the shotgun-nature of the wedding, and second Teri thought, but hoped she was wrong, because of Sean's hapa-haole heritage. *Well, tough*, Teri thought. *My son inherited his Hawai'ian/Japanese looks from me and his Irish temperament from Frank. So live with it, lady.* Meagan had been too pregnant, and too sick every day, to take the flight to the Big Island. So Teri had to be satisfied that she at least got to see them married before her granddaughter was born. Trixie Maile Anne Maegher. What a beautiful little girl. Though Teri had only seen pictures of her grand-daughter so far, Sean and Meagan had promised that they would bring Trixie over to the Big Island – maybe for her first birthday party next year.

"Teri? Teri?"

"Huh? Oh, sorry," Teri realized that Haunani had spoken to her, but she hadn't heard anything her mother had said.

"Back with us now?"

"Yes, Mom. I was just . . . thinking."

"Well maybe you better save the thinking for the car. It's almost five o'clock now. We have to be down in Kona in less than an hour. You don't want me driving too fast, do you?"

"God, no!" Teri said.

"Amen," Lori added.

"Okay, let's go then."

As they exited Lori's office Teri paused and looked back inside.

"This is the first time I've seen your new office, Lori. It's really nice."

"Yes, it used to be a conference room and had a much longer conference table. I had that moved out and this shorter one brought it. It'll work just fine until the owners decide to let me hire back those two assistant managers I had to let go." Lori's brow furrowed as she continued, "Besides, I had to get out of my old office. I kept seeing all the blood."

Teri and Lori hugged tightly for a very long moment, each remembering the tragic events from earlier in the year.

* * *

Haunani led the way out to the front of the hotel. A valet went off to get their car while the two women waited.

Haunani put her arm around her daughter's waist and turned toward her.

"Every day you get a little stronger, girl."

"Are you talking about the lua group work, or about my mental stability?"

Haunani kissed Teri lightly on the cheek. She released her daughter as the valet arrived with their car.

"Both, girl. Both," she said as she got in the driver's side and Teri took the shotgun position.

"Buckle up!" Haunani said with a grin as she pulled swiftly away from the curb and into the circular drive in front of the hotel.

CHAPTER TWENTY-THREE

Queen Ka`ahumanu Highway
On the way to Kona

Leaving the entrance road to the Queen's Beach Resort Hotel behind with a screech Haunani pulled out onto the Queen Ka`ahumanu Highway heading south toward Kona. It was quite evident that Haunani enjoyed her new car. She had taken delivery of a Toyota Highlander V6 4x4 in Super White with ivory cloth seats only seven weeks ago. Haunani made a point of having the car washed once a week and hosed the dust and dirt off it two or three times between washing, usually letting her speed on the road air-dry the car. Haunani was stopped three or four times every year for speeding along the highway to Kona. Each time her ploy, successful so far, was to remind the officer who stopped her that she knew his mother, had probably changed his diapers and would be sure and tell his mother how he had mistreated an old friend of hers. She had received over eight warnings so far but only one citation. That one citation had come when Haunani had been stopped two weeks previously for speeding. When the officer had stepped up to the window of her car and looked in, Haunani had asked forcefully, "Do you know who I am?" The officer had given her a wry smile and answered, "Yes, Auntie, I do. Do you know who I am?" Haunani's memory failed her for once. When she admitted that she didn't know who he was, he replied, "Auntie, I'm the officer who let you off last time you were speeding on this highway." He then proceeded to write her a citation that he delivered along with a warning to slow down.

Teri was remembering those recent events as, out of the corner of her eye, she watched the needle on the speedometer edge past seventy miles per hour.

"Mom?"

"Hush! If I don't hurry we're gonna be late. And I'm too old to do pushups or carry the ʻōlohe around on my back. Besides, if we're late we'll have to get one of the other students to tell us the password for the next lesson. And last time that big Japanese guy, Kenji, made me bake him two lilikoʻi pies as payment for the password."

"He's Hawaiʻian, Mom."

"Sure, but I know his mother and she's full-blood Japanese. Nice lady, really. Very short. Petite. But you know she still keeps her boys in line. I saw her tell Kenji one time that she had something to tell him, and when he bent down to listen to her, 'Crack!' right upside his head. She has one strong arm that one. Why, I bet . . ."

"Mom! Please watch the road!" Teri implored as the Highlander veered toward the center divide.

"Don't worry so much! I've been driving this road for over fifty years . . ."

"And I'd like to see us travel it for another fifty. Just watch where you're going, please?"

Haunani harrumphed, but focused her attention back onto the highway in front of them. Neither of them spoke for another five minutes.

* * *

"So, what do you think about Felicia coming over here?" Teri asked finally breaking the silence.

Getting no immediate reply Teri continued, "I think it's a good chance for us to get to know her better."

Haunani mulled that over for a minute before answering her daughter.

"Yes, could be good and could be not so good."

"What do you mean?"

"Just that I'm not so sure about that girl. Remember . . . how at first she said she couldn't come for Frank's funeral. Too busy taking exams at school."

78

"Yes, but be fair Mom. Jeremy begged off at first too. He said he couldn't take time away from his job because of that big merger with some other Internet powerhouse."

Teri tried not to let it show but she had been hurt greatly when it first appeared that both Jeremy and Felicia would be unable to attend Frank's funeral services. Jeremy and Felicia had only changed their plans after Haunani had gotten on the phone and berated Jeremy fiercely. Once the two of them had arrived on the island, however, Haunani had acted as if there had never been a thought that they wouldn't attend the funeral services.

Silence surrounded the two women for a few miles of driving. Haunani was the first to break that silence.

"All I know, Teri, is that if they love each other then it's fine with me. But they have to love each other. No good if only one of them is in love."

Teri turned to her mother.

"Mom? I never asked you before. How did you feel about my marrying Frank?"

Haunani laughed.

"That pupule Irishman? He was so crazy . . . crazy mad for you. You know, I knew he'd burn like heck in the sun over here. Could never tell if he was sunburned or just had too many beers." She turned her attention to Teri . . . and Teri gestured for Haunani to keep her eyes on the road. "But I knew from the minute I met him that you two were meant for each other. You made one perfect couple."

This time Teri couldn't hold them back. As tears streamed from her eyes her mother reached over and pulled Teri's head down onto her shoulder. Haunani blinked to clear her own eyes as she stared intensely at the road ahead. She'd failed once to protect her own family. She had no intention of ever failing again.

CHAPTER TWENTY-FOUR
Lua School

Haunani kept the Highlander flying along the Queen Ka`ahumanu Highway past the Kona International Airport until they turned mauka away from the ocean on Hina Lani Street. Not quite four miles farther along Hina Lani she turned right onto Halolani and, before reaching the junction with Hikimoe, pulled up in front of a single-story home that seemed to be made up primarily of whitewashed concrete blocks. The home sat somewhat below street level. There were already four pickup trucks in various states of disrepair, along with a Dodge Charger, whose license plate read "BCK OFF" and a Toyota Corolla of indeterminate years, parked along the street in front of the house. The Dodge Charger was the only one of the cars with plenty of room left around it. Wise people took no chances of denting that owner's car.

Haunani and Teri grabbed gym bags from the backseat of the Highlander and walked quickly down the steep driveway, through the open-air carport and toward a small gate in the six-foot-high flat white painted wooden fence that circled the house. Above the gate hung a small fisherman's net, and in the net rested a large stone collected from some upcountry stream. The net was tied to the beam above with a slipknot and one end of the slipknot rope ran down to where it was wrapped around a cleat rescued from a sailboat and screwed to the fence. One pull on the rope and anyone underneath the net would be flattened by the stone.

"Stop!" a guard commanded. To reinforce his command he brandished a club made out of a heavy piece of ironwood with a rock lashed to one end. That particular guard, and his club, always made Teri think of a comic strip caveman from her childhood. But she could never remember his name. The guard's authority wasn't enhanced by the fact that he was terribly thin with legs that looked like sticks poking out from his tight black shorts. Teri grinned at the sight of his legs and his hairless bare chest.

"Palani, it's us. C'mon, we're almost late," Teri said.

"Password!"

"Mokomoko!" Haunani said in a low but menacing voice as she made to walk past Palani.

Palani, who worked as a cook at a burger shop in Kona, had too high an opinion of his ability. He stepped in front of Haunani with his right hand outstretched, fingers pointing up. Haunani ran right into his hand letting it come to rest on her less than ample chest. She dropped her gym bag and at the same time placed both her palms onto the back of Palani's hand. Pressing his hand to her chest Haunani dropped to one knee as she bent forward. With his hand trapped Palani was forced to his knees and grimaced in pain as his elbow also moved toward the ground. Haunani kept up the pressure until Palani, unable to raise his left hand either, let go of his club and slapped his thigh with his free left hand in a signal of submission.

Haunani released Palani immediately, picked up her gym bag and, pushing open the gate, continued on into the yard with Teri following her.

Behind her Palani retrieved his rock-topped club and rose back up onto his feet.

"Shit, Haunani, I just doing my job," he complained.

A small smile flitted across Haunani's lips as she and Teri ducked into a makeshift changing room made up of old sheets hung off a clothesline.

Teri saw the smile and, frowning, shook her head at her mother when Haunani met her gaze.

"Oh, c'mon girl, you know Palani thinks he's better than any woman could ever be."

Teri stripped off her regular clothes and donned black gym shorts with a red pictograph of a warrior brandishing a club just above where the shorts ended on her thigh. She pulled a black teeshirt over her head as she replied, "I know he does. But you didn't need to be so rough. If the others had seen Palani would have been humiliated."

81

"Teaches him a lesson," Haunani muttered to herself as she changed into identical clothing.

Leaving their regular clothes tucked into their gym bags, Teri and Haunani slipped through an opening between two sheets and walked barefoot around and into the back yard of the house. This area served as the lua school. After last year's tragic events Haunani had pushed Teri into joining the lua school in order to learn the ancient Hawai`ian fighting art. She had reminded Teri that in order to take over the family responsibility of guarding the secret hiding place of the bones of Queen Ka`ahumanu, Kamehameha's favorite wife, Teri needed to be able to physically defend that secret.

"I know you're intelligent and mentally tough," Haunani had said, *"but you also need to be physically tough. Koakane's lua school with help you with that."*

She had also pushed Koakane to accept Teri into the school. It was the one time that Koakane hadn't selected a student by himself. He still wondered at times why he had taken Teri in to his school. He knew that Haunani had persuaded him – he just didn't know why he had given in to her.

Teri had met Koakane last year before . . . *Before I lost Frank and before I almost lost Shari and my mom*, she remembered. Koakane worked up at the observatory as a handyman, and also danced hula at the Pono Family Hale luaus. Teri remembered how strong and supple he had looked wearing just a malo the first time she saw him. But that memory also brought back memories of Frank, who had been at that luau, and she struggled to separate the two memories.

Rounding the corner into the larger back yard, surrounded on three sides by a high fence, Teri and Haunani paused and turned toward an old table. Painted black to cover the nicks and scrapes of years of service, an ancient kapa cloth runner lay ready to receive the deities of the lua school and various sacred ferns and flowers that would be placed there when one or more of the students was judged ready to graduate. Teri and Haunani bowed once to the empty altar before moving quietly toward the practice area where Koakane was already waiting with the other students of the lua school.

CHAPTER TWENTY-FIVE

Haunani and Teri walked over to where Koakane stood with four other men, loosely forming a circle which Haunani and Teri completed as they took their places. The men all wore black gym shorts with the petroglyph emblem, but no shirts.

Palani stood to Teri's right giving a stink-eye look at Haunani for her earlier treatment of him. On his right stood Brandon, a security guard for the Royal Kona Hotel far down Ali'i Drive. Then came Koakane, his skin glistening in the late afternoon sun. Teri found herself fixated by his rippling muscles, taut stomach and the shock of black hair on his head. The hair on his head was the only hair she could see on his body. *He must shave himself to get that smooth*, Teri thought. Koakane was only as tall as Frank had been, about five ten, and probably weighed the same. But his strength was evident. What wasn't readily apparent was the training that Koakane had undergone since he was only four years old. With two calabash Japanese uncles to guide him Koakane had studied judo, jiu-jitsu, and aikido for over twenty years before he found his own 'ōlohe with whom he studied lua for another twenty years before starting his own school. Beside Koakane stood Vincent, the youngest of the group, with sun-bleached hair and a great smile. Vincent worked at a surf shop and spent most of his free hours out on the ocean catching waves – and sweet young tourist girls. In sharp contrast next to Vincent, and beside Haunani, stood Francisco Na'ale. Francisco stood immobile like a rock, and resembled one. He was undoubtedly the darkest-skinned of the group and most likely the strongest. Teri could still feel the bruises on her hip and thigh from working out with Francisco at their last training session.

Koakane looked from Teri to Haunani. Teri waited to see if he would make the two of them do pushups in front of the rest of the students today. She thought about protesting if he did order them, even though she knew she would have to obey his orders. But they hadn't been late. Everyone else had just happened to be early today.

Haunani stared back without concern at Koakane.

Koakane made up his mind.

"Ho'omaka," he commanded directing the group to begin. He led his students in stretching and loosening-up exercises. A prelude to today's training in the art of fighting – Hawai`ian-style.

CHAPTER TWENTY-SIX

Two hours later with practice completed the circle was re-formed. All the students were sweating profusely, the hair on their heads matted, everyone's gym shorts, and the women's teeshirts, soaked as if their wearers had just come out of the ocean.

Koakane stood at his place in the circle looking exactly the same as when he had begun today's practice. Teri hated him for looking so composed when they all looked so ragged and wrung out by their work today.

"Next month . . . the password is 'aumakua. If you do not have an 'aumakua, a family spirit to guide you through this life, then you should meditate and fast in order to find your 'aumakua." Looking up at the roof over his carport Koakane gestured at a pueo who sat there grooming its feathers in preparation for tonight's hunt. "My family's 'aumakua has watched over us and guided us for generations."

Koakane turned back to his group, folded his right fist inside his left hand and, when all the students had done likewise, bowed from the waist. His students bowed back to him, but lower.

Straightening up the group split apart as they began to go their separate ways.

"Teri?"

Teri paused and turned back as Koakane walked over to where she stood. Haunani looked back once before continuing on to the makeshift changing room.

"Yes, 'ōlohe?"

"Nah, just Koakane now. Or even Bradley . . . but not Brad. Bradley was my mom's way of making sure that I'd always remember my dad. We lost him during the Korean War."

"I'm sorry," was all Teri could think of to say.

"Yeah, well . . . anyway, I just wanted to . . . to say that you did a whole lot better today. You're looking really good . . . in practice."

"Mahalo, 'ōlo – Koakane."

"And, uh, well . . . well keep it up."

"I will. I need to get changed. My mom will want to get us home."

"Yeah, right. Okay, see you. Aloha," and with that Koakane walked away and went in the back door of his house.

Teri finished changing behind the sheets on the drying rack. She thought to herself, *That was one of the strangest conversations I've ever had with the 'ōlohe.*

* * *

Now changed into their regular clothes, but still both in dire need of a shower, Haunani and Teri climbed back into the Toyota Highlander, and opened the windows. As they pulled away from the house Teri admired the view over the rooftops and out to the sea. She wondered if Koakane took time to enjoy the view. She wondered if he even could enjoy the view what with all the land in between his house and the ocean being gobbled up by new housing developments and boxy warehouses with multitudes of small businesses.

Haunani eased the car out into the street, down to the intersection where she turned left on Hikimoe Street and then left again on Hina Lani heading then onto the Queen's highway and north to the family hale.

"Mom? What do you suppose this all looked like back before?"

"Before what?"

"Before when it was just the native Hawai`ians living here?"

Haunani cast a quick glance out to sea where the sun was just heading down for its nightly dip into the ocean.

"Beautiful. Just beautiful back then."

CHAPTER TWENTY-SEVEN

Teri and Haunani were the only two members of the lua school to leave Koakane's house after the training was over. As they pulled away in Haunani's Highlander several other cars that had been waiting back up the street slid forward and came down to park closer to Koakane's driveway. By ones and twos other men got out of those cars and strolled down the driveway, through the gate and around to the backyard.

Koakane had changed into a pair of worn jeans and a dark brown muscle tee whose front carried the message in bright yellow letters – **HAWAI'IAN HOME = HAWAI'IAN LAND**. Assisted by the male members of the lua school, who had also changed into their street clothes, Koakane was pulling together a mixed group of chairs – plastic garden, folding, wicker, wood – and arranging them in a rough circle. On a folding six-foot picnic table under the eaves of the house he had already set out a large bowl of taro chips and two slightly smaller bowls of salsa and guacamole all covered in plastic wrap. Next to those was a stack of small wooden salad bowls, cracks and dents revealing their age. In a cooler under the table four six-packs of soda kept cold on a thick layer of ice cubes. On one end of the picnic table sat a small black cd player, plugged into an extension cord that ran through a window and into the kitchen.

The men from the cars outside joined the lua school students in finishing the setup, then they all moved to stand in front of the various chairs. It was clear that some of the group had their favorite chair. Francisco's was an old overstuffed armchair with holes in the seat and back covered by an old beach towel. One of the non-lua school men pretended to sit down in Francisco's chair. He moved quickly to another chair when a low growl issued from Francisco's throat. Palani laughed at the byplay.

Another of the men not from the lua school took a white plastic chair, shifted it slightly, drew out a six-pack of beer from a supermarket paper bag and stashed the beer under the chair. As he straightened up he found Koakane regarding him intently.

"Hey, for laters," the man explained shrugging his shoulders at the same time.

"Better next time you leave the beer in your car."

"Yeah, sure, Koakane. I'll remember next time."

Seeing that everyone had secured a chair and that they were all standing and waiting, Koakane stepped over to the whitewashed back wall of his house and carefully removed a large white sheet hanging there. Under the sheet, fastened to the wall, was a four-foot by six-foot Hawai`ian flag. To the left of the flag was a carved wooden plaque with the motto *Malama Pono O Ka 'Āina.* On the opposite side of the flag was a similarly carved wooden plaque with *Imua Lanakila* on it.

Koakane pushed the play button on the cd player and the group stood quietly as Iz's voice rang out and filled the backyard with his great rendition of *Living in a Sovereign Land.* As the song ended and the applause from the audience who had been there when the song was recorded replaced the music Koakane clicked off the player. He took his seat and all the others followed his lead.

"All right, this meeting of Malama Pono O Ka 'Āina is officially open." Koakane looked around the circle. Besides the members of his lua school the circle now included Greyson, a blend of Native American Indian and Hawai`ian and English, who worked as a tour guide for a sea kayak company. Next to him sat Chad, a younger man who worked as an assistant hotel engineer at a big hotel along the Kona waterfront. Sitting next to Francisco was Peter Sakamoto, a bartender from the Queen's Beach Resort Hotel. Peter always made it a point to sit at least one chair away from a fellow worker at the hotel, Keoki Akane, who drove a shuttle bus for the hotel. Keoki frequently drove guests from the hotel up to the Pono Family Hale to attend the luau held there. Keoki had hooked one leg under his chair in order to keep a foot in touch with his six-pack of beer. After all, it was *his* beer. One chair remained empty.

"I have good news today," Koakane announced. "You all know that since our fellow member, Lalepa, was found in the ocean back in February, I have been looking for a new member to take his place in our group. That's been very hard. Lalepa was dedicated to our cause – to bringing Hawai`ian sovereignty back to these islands. He knew this island as well as anyone ever did. He was truly at home wherever he went on the aina."

Koakane paused and looked over the group.

"We will probably never know why he died," and Koakane looked blandly first at Keoki and then at Peter, "nor will we know whether or not he completed his last assignment. Will we?"

Peter leaned forward in his chair and spoke earnestly to Koakane, "Hey, I told you already. Yeah, I was supposed go with Lalepa that day an' put the iwi back. Lalepa said he knew a place where no one ever going find 'em. But . . ."

"But your girlfriend needed you to drive her up to Hawi to see her mother."

"Right. She no can drive since she got another DUI . . . other than around town a little," a couple of the other members of the group shook their heads at the thought of Peter's girlfriend driving illegally around Kona. Even legally most of them didn't think his girlfriend should be driving anywhere.

"So you called Keoki?" Koakane asked turning to look at that member of the group.

"Right, I call him and leave a message on his machine for him to go with Lalepa."

"And?" Koakane asked Keoki.

"Hey, I get sick. No can go wit' Lalepa. But I figure he already go by the time I call since he no pick up the phone."

"You got *sick*," Koakane stated.

Keoki flinched a little, but responded, "Yeah, I no can help! I always think maybe was the luau food from da night before. They don't finish everything at da luau, an' I take some kal-bi an' some teri chicken home, an' some other stuff. Coulda been da potato-mac salad . . . or maybe some lomi-lomi salmon . . . or even–"

"Right, we get it Keoki. You had too much to eat so you blew off helping Lalepa. Or maybe you had too much to drink?"

"Nyah, only one six-pack after I get home. For wash da food down you know? No, I think maybe was da potato-mac salad cuz–"

Koakane waved his hand through the air batting aside Keoki's words.

"Enough, it doesn't matter. Neither one of you were there to help your brother fulfill his responsibility to our group." Koakane sighed heavily as he looked first down at the ground and then over at the Hawai`ian flag and mottos on the wall.

"Lalepa must have gone out by himself, and somehow he wound up in the ocean . . . battered by the rocks. Alone with no one to help him."

Koakane inhaled deeply, let the air out and placed both hands on his thighs. Leaning forward he looked slowly around the group.

"I have a replacement for Lalepa, a new member of our group, to introduce to you today. Manu! Come on out!" Koakane called toward the house.

Everyone swiveled in their chairs as the kitchen screen door creaked open and then slammed shut. A tall man came walking confidently toward the group. He was a light mocha with thick curly black hair. His mouth held a tentative smile and his eyes were bright – and intelligent. He wore a teeshirt with a motto that read *So Many Books . . . So Little Time.*

Koakane stood up and ushered the man into the middle of the group. As he reached the center of the circle all the members stood. Koakane placed his hand on the man's shoulder, and turned slowly along with the man to face, in turn, each member of the group.

"This is Manu. He moved over here from O'ahu a couple of months ago. He works down along Ali'i Drive in the Four-Eyed Owl bookstore. I've talked with him and I'm satisfied that he will be a valuable addition to our group."

Koakane dropped his hand from Manu's shoulder.

"Manu, these are the members of Malama Pono O Ka 'Āina. In joining us you are promising to work steadfastly to restore

Hawai'ian Sovereignty to these islands. We are not a violent group . . . as some are. But we will not stand by idly as our people dwindle and their heritage is taken from them. We will work to reclaim our people's homeland. To bring self-rule back to our people."

Koakane paused to let all the men feel the impact of his words. He looked around the circle again, and then back to Manu.

"Are you prepared to be a full member of this group, to work for our goals, and to keep secret those things that we discuss and plan here?"

In a soft bass voice Manu replied, "I promise all this with all my heart. And I thank you all for admitting me to your group."

Much backslapping and handshaking and congratulations followed this induction of Manu to the group. Everyone relaxed for a few minutes. The sodas were distributed and bowls filled with taro chips and dips. Keoki reached under his chair to retrieve a beer from his six-pack, but the look he received from Koakane persuaded him to settle for a soda.

Several people were interested in the latest goings-on in Francisco Na'ale's life. Francisco was not the only member of the group who had made official application with the Department of Hawai'ian Homelands, but he was the group member who had applied the longest time ago.

"So, howzit going with your application?" asked Brandon.

"Slow, brah, slow. Shit, da buggahs tell me da other day dey change my numbah."

"What you mean *change your number?*"

"I mean dey move me back on da list. I lose maybe fifteen places."

"How come?"

"Say it's 'cuz other people no can take da house or land dey get. So dey give dat up an' come back on da list fo' wait an' try again fo' some other place."

"So how come dey no go to da end of da list?"

"'Cuz dey been on da list already, so go back at da front."

"Buggah!"

"Right on! But I no can do nothing 'bout it."

Since Brandon was also on the last, and much farther back than Francisco, this news was pretty depressing. And since his wife was Chinese/Portuguese their kids were much less than fifty percent and would have no chance to even get on the list. He still hoped that he had a chance for a vacant lot down in the development area of La 'I 'Opua in Kona.

Brandon thought that maybe sometime their group should get more involved in dealing with the Department of Hawai'ian Homelands. Maybe even get one of their members on the Board there.

* * *

When everyone had their refreshments Koakane called the group back together for the rest of their meeting. Koakane related his continuing efforts to get the local papers to use the group's full name in articles rather than just calling them Malama Pono, or even, as one particularly reviled columnist did, simply M.P.

"That guy just so lazy!" Vincent said shaking his head.

Koakane then went on to talk about activities on O'ahu by other groups that their group supported, and about how those activities might affect them.

Francisco brought up the matter of the local police making him take down the Hawai'ian flag and banner that he regularly put up on his truck when he parked on the weekends opposite the exit from the Kona airport.

"You know, I told them was my day off an' I can do what I want. I'm not blocking traffic or nothing. But they just say I can't park along the side of the highway an' '*Deestrak Peoples*'. Shit, like they make the guys selling mangos and bananas move their trucks?"

"You get their names?" Koakane asked.

When Francisco nodded Koakane went on, "Okay, give 'em to me and I'll talk with Skipper." Seeing puzzlement on Manu's face Koakane explained, "Skipper Madison. Haole lawyer down by Captain Cook. Do-gooder type, but does pro-bono stuff for us – free stuff."

The group talked about various other issues for another twenty minutes. At times members would wander over to the picnic table to refill their bowls or to pop open another soda.

Eventually Koakane said, "Okay, only two things left for us today. First, I think you all heard that they discovered iwi up at the Queen's Beach Resort Hotel."

"Yeah, it's turned into a big deal up there. At first the contractor tried hide some of the bones, but then kept finding more and more so had to report it," Peter spoke with an air of importance having so much inside information.

"Uh-huh, well, the big deal is getting even bigger. The hotel is calling in an archeological investigation team to check out the site and to help determine what to do with the iwi."

Koakane paused and looked over the group again. He smiled with satisfaction.

"And guess who the hotel has agreed to bring in to be a part of the investigation . . . and to help decide what to do with the iwi after they're uncovered?"

"Us?" Greyson asked.

"Yep!" Koakane answered with even more satisfaction. "Us! Our group gets to be part of this. Just as we've been asking at other sites around the island for the past three years. They're finally going to recognize that we have a legitimate right to participate in this undertaking. After all, they are our ancestors' remains," he paused briefly. "Of course, the fact that our lawyer spoke with them, and the fact that I mentioned that if they refused us access we might have to set up a picket line outside the entrance to the hotel . . . well, those things helped persuade them."

Koakane looked around at the men seated in a circle.

"They won't let our whole group in, but they will let three of us on site. So I'm going to need two of you to assist me."

All hands rose high in the air.

"Okay, Peter . . . Keoki, put your hands down. Since you both work at the hotel we're not going to make you a part of this. I don't want you involved in anything that might affect your jobs."

Both men said that they understood, even though they acted disappointed.

" Let's see, we don't want anybody to lose any pay over this so that means Francisco, you're out, and Greyson, and Palani, Chad and Vincent . . . all you guys would have to take off to be in this. So that leaves Brandon, you mostly work nights, right? And Manu, even though you're new this will give you some experience with our group. Plus, if I remember right, your boss is pretty flexible about your hours."

Koakane paused to marshal his thoughts.

"Koakane?" Francisco spoke up from where he sat, "You suppose that when you get all this worked out with the hotel and these archeologists that there will be a re-burial ceremony?"

"That's the path I'm thinking right now."

"Well, if there's a re-burial ceremony then could we all come to that? Maybe set it up for a weekend when we're not working . . . if not maybe an evening?" Francisco asked.

"I think that's very possible," Koakane answered. "In fact, Francisco, don't you have an uncle who's a kahu? If we have a re-burial ceremony then we'll need a priest to do the blessing and the chanting."

"Sure, got my uncle Clayton. I'll sound him out, but cannot promise anything."

"Good. Now, we have one last item to deal with," Koakane got up as he spoke, stepped over to the picnic table and pulled a small box out from under the table.

"These came in this week," and opening the box Koakane took out a handful of brightly-colored shiny new bumper stickers. He held one up for all the group to see.

In solid black letters on a bright red background was the saying, *"I AIN'T NEVER HAD AN UNCLE NAMED SAM!"*

The bumper stickers were soon distributed with instructions not only to put them on the groups' own vehicles, but also on friends' vehicles.

"But only if they say okay first. Don't just go slapping them on any car you see!"

Everybody agreed to the restriction.

With some difficulty Koakane calmed the happy group down and got them returned to standing in front of their chairs. Stepping over to the cd player once more he pushed the play button again.

This time the cd of the Peter Moon Band came on playing *Song of Sovereignty* from their Greatest Hits Collection II album.

At the end of the song Koakane bade the group farewell and wished them all safe travel.

As the group left Koakane began to clean up his back yard.

Manu paused at the gate and looked back at the man now covering his group's plaques and the Hawai'ian flag. A small conflicted wave of emotion crossed his face as he turned and headed toward his car.

* * *

Koakane finished the cleaning up after lua school and his meeting with the men of Malama Pono O Ka 'Āina. He was tired and knew that he better get some sleep since he had a number of jobs to complete up at the observatory tomorrow. Remembering tomorrow's schedule made him shake his head. He had forgotten to get gas for his car today. That made one more early morning chore since it wouldn't do to run out of gas on the road up to the observatory.

Before going back into the house to prepare for bed he looked up at the night sky. With no streetlights up here the stars were much more visible, though not as visible as from the top of Mauna Kea. But it was a pretty night . . . the kind of night that could be spent sitting pleasantly out in the backyard, gazing at the stars while holding a beautiful woman's hand.

Koakane wondered what Teri was doing right now . . . then reluctantly pushed that thought out of his head. He shivered a bit, amazed at how much cooler it was now that the sun had gone down.

Koakane turned, stepped over to the kitchen door and put his hand on the handle. As he prepared to open the door the call of a pueo beginning its nightly hunt cause him to look back at the sky.

"Good hunting," he called out. He didn't know whether this particular pueo was his family's aumakua, but it didn't hurt to be respectful to all the owls in the neighborhood.

Koakane followed the circling owl with his eyes and was just able to see over the corner of the front fence that two cars belonging to members of his group had yet to leave the street. With a shake of his head and a determined set to his mouth Koakane turned away from his kitchen door.

CHAPTER TWENTY-EIGHT

Back in his dusty green Kia Sephia, Keoki finally popped open one of the beers from his six-pack and downed it in one long swallow. He belched with satisfaction as he crumpled the can and dropped it on the passenger side floorboard. He inserted his key in the ignition, but instead of turning it reached for a second beer can.

The second beer went down in three swallows with a short interval between each swallow. The second crumpled can followed the first.

Keoki popped open the third can but just sat there holding the cold can as he looked out over the town of Kona. *Look at all those lucky buggahs down there! None of them probably have to bust their humps like I do!* He took a swallow of the beer and held the cold can up to the side of his head for a half minute. He balanced the half empty can on the cracked dashboard and slouched down in his seat. He tried to get comfortable but the duct tape covering the long slash down the seat back made that difficult. Still, he was somewhat satisfied with this car. After all, it was a 2001 model. The newest car he had ever owned. And it had only cost him fifteen hundred dollars . . . he pushed aside the memory that he still owed a little over a thousand of that amount.

Shoving his hand deep into his right hand pants pocket Keoki pulled out a small roll of bills. Skipping over the one's on the outside he counted through the five's, ten's, and twenty's. At the very core he located his last remaining one hundred dollar bill. Adding it in he came to a total of three hundred and ten dollars . . . not counting the one's. Through the growing beer fog he reviewed things coming up that he couldn't avoid paying for. The total of those things exceeded the roll of cash in his hand. And a lot of things that he enjoyed weren't included in the things that he would be forced to pay for.

Keoki shoved the roll back into his pocket and reached for the beer can on the dashboard. His fingers brushed it and knocked it off the dashboard and onto the floorboard at his feet. Beer sloshed out of the can and soaked into the old piece of carpet he'd put down as a floor mat. Keoki managed to save one small swallow from the can, and he drank that even as he cursed his bad luck.

Three crumpled cans on the floor and only three left in his six-pack. It was enough to make Keoki think seriously, though that was somewhat difficult in his current state.

Nothing else to do . . . I guess I'll have to . . .

A knock on his halfway rolled-up driver's side window snapped him into an upright position.

"Hey, Keoki? You okay? How come you're still here?"

"Oh, hey Koakane, uhh, I just got . . . got thinking . . . you know . . . just thinking. Looking out at all the lights. Makes you think, right?" Keoki didn't bother to roll down the window.

Koakane looked in at Keoki with narrowed eyes.

"You okay to drive?"

"Sure, no problem, I had one beer while I was thinking. That's all."

Koakane saw full beers on the seat next to Keoki, but couldn't see the crumpled empty cans on the floor of the passenger side in the darkness.

"Okay. Okay, well, see you then, okay?"

Keoki turned the key in the ignition.

"Yeah, sure, aloha Koakane," he said as he put the car in gear and began to pull away from the curb.

"Hey, Keoki, put your lights on!"

"Oh? Yeah, sure. 'Night now, Koakane. Bye."

As he reached the intersection at the end of the street Keoki looked back in the rearview mirror at Koakane standing there watching him drive off.

Keoki waved. Speaking softly to himself he muttered, "Bye, Big Shot. You think you know it all. Ha, you don't know half of what you should."

Keoki sped up as he turned onto Hikimoe Street and turned left at the intersection onto Hina Lani without stopping. He flipped his middle finger at the strident horn from the car he cut off.

Stupid buggah, get outta my way!

Keoki thought about driving straight back to his place. He decided against that and thought maybe he'd just stop off at a little bar he knew. After all, his wahine would smell the beer on his breath from the few that he'd already had, and then she'd be off again on his drinking. So what the hell, might as well stop and have a few more. Might as well be feeling good if he was going to catch it again for his drinking.

Keoki accelerated down the street. He kept close to the centerline in order to keep from wandering off to the side.

CHAPTER TWENTY-NINE

Two houses back from where Keoki was parked Peter Sakamoto sat parked along the curb in his yellow Toyota Corona with the dented right front fender. He was mulling over the same basic problem.

Where the hell am I gonna get some money quick?

The issue of money loomed larger since last week's scare. His long-time girlfriend Nani had, for two whole days, been positive that she had missed her period . . . and that she was pregnant. And she'd been happy about it! By the time she had finally gotten her period she'd already made a guest list for the wedding and informed Peter that when the baby came they would have to move to a bigger place in a nicer neighborhood. And no more parking his car on the lawn!

Damn her! Why the hell it always gotta be my responsibility? Why don't she just take some pills? But Peter heard the answer in his mind even as he asked himself the question for the two hundredth time. And it was always the same answer, *"If I take those pills they maybe can do bad things to my body. And I should chance that just so you don't need to put on a rubber? Hell no, Peter! Hell no!"*

Peter always refrained from telling Nani that if she did get pregnant having a baby was going to do more bad things to her body than a few birth control pills ever could. And now that he knew she actually welcomed the idea of getting pregnant – Well, he needed to be more prepared. Yep, a nice stash of cash was the way to go. Then if it ever looked like he was gonna be a daddy for sure – well, with enough cash he could not only split the island for the mainland but also be able to set himself up in comfort there. A couple hundred for the plane ticket and at least a thousand – no, make that two thousand – to get himself a place and tide him over until he could score there.

All of which brought him back to his original problem. *Where the hell am I gonna get a lot of money quick?*

Peter was so deep in thought that he hit his head on the roof inside the car when Koakane knocked on the window.

Peter rolled the window down all the way to allow Koakane to lean in.

"You okay, brother?"

"Oh, yeah, sure. I was . . . uh, jus' thinkin'. Got a few things on my mind lately."

"Anything I can help with?"

Peter opened his mouth, and then closed it again. Finally he said, "No, nothing you could help with. But thanks."

"All right, then. You better get on home, Peter. I don't want Lani calling me and getting on my case about keeping you so late."

"Yeah, yeah. I'm going now. See you."

Starting up his car Peter looked ahead to see that Keoki had already left and that he was the last one there. *I better get going. Nani gonna bust my chops already for being this late.*

Peter paused when he got to the intersection, reached down and retrieved a small leather bag from under the seat. He took out a loosely-wrapped cigarette and lit it. The first hit of the pakalolo seemed to push all of his problems out the window.

"Good shit this," he said to no one in particular as he took a second hit, held it in his lungs and, upon releasing it, put the Corona in gear and pulled out through the intersection. A wide grin split his face, "Awful good shit!"

CHAPTER THIRTY
Pono Family Hale
Mother's Day, May 13, 2007

"Shall we make a list of what we need to take care of before they arrive?" Teri asked her mother.

Haunani put the small plate that held her freshly toasted sourdough bread down beside her larger plate with the poached egg and two sausages on it. She buttered her toast and spread some thick guava jam on it while she thought over the upcoming visit.

"Have we got that much to do that we need to make a list?"

"Well, I just don't want us to skip anything and have to rush at the last minute."

Haunani cut into her poached egg with her fork, brought a piece to her mouth and then, putting down her fork, took a bite out of one piece of toast. She took her time chewing and swallowing, and when she had finished took a sip of unsweetened green tea from the thick mug to the left of her plate.

"Okay, so you want us to have a list? Then I think we should have a list. You go ahead and make it and then we'll check it over together," Haunani spoke mildly as she cut one of her sausages into pieces.

Teri opened her mouth to protest being given all the work, realized that she set herself up again for this chore, and then pictured how unappetizing her open mouth with food inside must look. She quickly shut it again.

"All right, I'll sit down later and make a list. But you need to check it over to be sure I don't leave anything out."

Haunani nodded agreement.

The two women ate in silence for a while.

Teri was the first to break that silence.

"We need to go over to the hotel later." Getting no response from Haunani, Teri continued, "Lori is treating us to dinner at the Plumeria Room. Shari said she'd join us."

Haunani continued eating.

"C'mon, Mom, it's Mother's Day. We all want to be with you and have a little party."

"Shari wants to be with me?"

"Mom! She's just a little . . . depressed . . . upset. I mean, she lost her husband and then lost their condo in Vegas and had to move back here. She's got a right to be a little . . . a little – "

Haunani looked up into Teri's eyes.

"And you? You have a right also."

"I'm handling it. I still have Sean . . . and Meagan . . . and Trixie. That's more than Shari has."

"Shari knows you have more than she has."

Haunani's words struck home with Teri. She did have more than Shari. How much did that bother Shari? It had been her sister Liz's jealousy that had brought tragedy on the family last year, including personal tragedy for Shari. *I don't try to have more than my sisters, and I've lost just as much as they have. Oh, my head hurts.*

As Teri rubbed her forehead Haunani looked upon her youngest daughter with compassion. Pushing back in her chair Haunani got up and stood behind Teri. She began to massage the stiffness out of Teri's shoulders.

Teri resisted Haunani's efforts for a minute, and then yielded.

"Oh, that feels so good, Mom. But you're the one who should be getting the massage. It's your Mother's Day."

"You're a mother, too. Relax."

Instead of relaxing, Teri jumped up from her chair.

"That's it! That's what we'll do!"

"Huh, what are you talking about?"

But Teri had already rushed across the room, picked up the phone and was dialing.

Haunani shrugged her shoulders and set about clearing away the breakfast dishes. She heard Teri talking in the background and just about the time she finished with the dishes Teri hung up the phone.

"Okay, Mom, get dressed. We're going to the hotel."

"Why so early? Dinner's not for hours yet."

"Right, but we are both going to get massages. In fact, Lori said she'd join us. And she's going to call Shari and see if she wants one too. Wouldn't that be great? All four of us getting massages out on that small terrace that they use there? And we can have Mai Tais or wine spritzers or whatever we want! And Lori said that instead of going out to dinner, she'll cancel the reservations, and we'll have a couple of pupu platters sent over there. It'll be wonderful! A real Mother's Day Celebration!

Haunani had to admit it sounded like a terrific treat. A massage would certainly relieve all the aches and pains that were the result of yesterday's lua training.

Teri was frustrated when Haunani took so long to get ready. But Haunani insisted on showering, and washing her hair, and putting on just a drop of her best cologne.

After all, she might know the mothers of the various masseuses.

* * *

While Haunani showered, Teri thought she would take one last look to be sure everything was in order for their guests. The bedroom that Felicia would share with Teri was already in perfect order. It would be tight with the twin bed that she and her mom had added to accommodate Felicia, but it would certainly give Teri a chance to come to know Felicia better. Teri thought that all she needed to do there now was to pick some fresh flowers from the garden for the vase on the dresser.

She went back up the hallway to the room the two men would be sleeping in. The room that had been hers and Franks' bedroom. There were two twin beds in there now, the queen bed having been moved to Teri's room after Frank's funeral. Both beds were made up and ready for the weary travelers. She checked the dresser; all the drawers were empty, plenty of room for both men to put away their clothes. Teri turned toward the door . . . and then forced herself back to the closet. She slid one of the closet doors back. Frank's golf clubs and the heavy canvas bag that he put the clubs in whenever they flew anywhere stood in the corner of the closet. Well, they didn't take up that much room so they could probably stay here. She slid back the other door and her heart caught in her throat. An old aloha shirt hung there. The shirt had been light blue once, but something had stained the shoulders, the entire front and part of the back of the shirt. Something dark. It was evident that someone had tried to wash out the stain, and had been only partly successful. Whatever had soaked the shirt had sunk in deeply and dried before the shirt was washed.

Teri reached into the closet and took the shirt, hanger and all, down. She gazed at the shirt for a long time before bringing it close to her face. Teri buried her face in the shirt trying to inhale its smell . . . but while the stain remained the familiar smell of the shirt was gone. Tears started in her eyes and ran slowly down her cheeks. She couldn't bear to part with the shirt . . . but she also couldn't bear to keep it in her closet where she would see it all the time. So it was that she came in once every morning to hold Frank's shirt to her face and try to get a faint whiff of his smell. It was almost more than she could bear   . . . but she felt that she couldn't go on without this morning ritual.

Teri slowly returned the shirt on its hanger to the closet rod. She slid it far back into the corner where it wouldn't be in anyone's way.

As she closed the closet she heard her mother call and quickly answered her.

"Yes, Mom, I'm coming. I'll be right there."

CHAPTER THIRTY-ONE

The wiry man had his own way of celebrating Mother's Day. He went out to his carport, retrieved a deteriorating cardboard box from the very back of a high shelf and took it back into the apartment. Clearing a space on the coffee table that had cost him only three dollars at a local thrift store, he began pulling all manner of ancient articles out of the box. Memorabilia from his high school days. Days when he remembered himself as a big man on campus. A real stud. It was really wonderful how selective his memory could be.

Finally he found the items he was looking for. An old instant camera – one pack of film, twelve exposures – and enough flash bulbs to use all twelve exposures in a dark cave.

He forgot about the camera for a short while when he found some of the photographs he had taken with it. They were hidden deep in the old box and wrapped in a gym sock, unwashed still and with a large hole in the heel. The photographs showed a very plain-looking, very young wahine. He remembered her now. She had been a freshman when he was a senior. Not so pretty, but really stacked when you got her clothes off. A really wild wahine, too! They'd cut classes and driven out to Punalu'u beach one day. He brought the instant camera and film. Nobody around at the far end of the beach so he'd been able to talk her into taking off her top for some photos. Then they'd found a green sea turtle up above the surf line, taking a nap. He'd suggested that she pose with the turtle, so she did. Sat on it. Lay on top of it. All sorts of poses. Then that couple came along and yelled at the two of them. Said they were bothering the turtle. Big guy. Where'd he get off telling him and his girl to get the hell off the beach?

He grinned thinking of how they *had* gotten off the beach, but how in leaving he'd taken time to urinate through the open window of the man's car. And had ripped off the car's radio antenna. That had probably taught the man not to mess around with him.

Good memories.

But he had to get going. He re-wrapped the pictures and hid them back in the box. No sense in taking them inside where they might be found. Put the box back in the carport high up on the shelf. Then he grabbed a flashlight, checked it to be sure that it had good batteries, took a bottle of water out of the refrigerator, and wrapped everything together in a small daypack. Picking up his car keys and closing the door behind him he could feel the butterflies starting to flutter in his stomach.

* * *

Traffic was easy since most people were either out at a restaurant or sitting around the house celebrating Mother's Day. It didn't take long for him to get to the Kazumura lava tube. As far as he could tell he was alone here today. Still, he looked around carefully to see if anyone was following him before he entered the tube. Once inside he took out his flashlight and set out for the burial chamber. He hoped that no one else had found it since the last time he was here.

* * *

Shivering from the cool air inside the tube, and from the silence that pressed down on him, he made his way through the tube carefully. His markers were still there, revealed in the beam of his flashlight. No do-gooders had removed the trash yet. A few more visits and he could probably take them away himself and just rely on his memory.

Sooner than he thought he arrived at the burial chamber. He flicked off his flashlight and peered into the darkness trying to see if anyone was following him. No other lights. No other movement. No other sounds – except for his rapid breathing.

He slipped into the burial chamber and turned on his flashlight again. It was better with the light on.

Everything was just as he remembered it. No one else had been here in the interim.

Taking out the old instant camera he loaded the film and snapped on a flashbulb. Aiming at the old sennit casket he pressed the button on the camera and was relieved when the flashbulb went off filling the burial chamber briefly with intense light. The camera spit out the picture and he waited impatiently for it to develop.

Blotches and streaks made the picture useless. Damn old film.

He tried another and the blotches and streaks were much less noticeable, in fact he could almost see the casket this time.

The third try was the charm. The picture turned out fine. Black and white, but still quite clear.

The wiry man took picture after picture of the items remaining in the burial chamber. With these pictures he could go to the antique dealer and bargain without having to take the relics along with him. Less chance of getting caught. Probably jack up his prices too.

He'd taken pictures of everything in the burial chamber and still had one picture left in the camera. Looking around he saw the mummy wrapped in its silk robe. Why not!

With more courage than he thought he possessed, the wiry man gently pulled the robe back from the mummy's face. He wondered briefly why this dead man had become a mummy while the man on the floor in front of the casket had been reduced to bones. Shrugging his shoulders he composed the picture, careful to include the mummy's face along with the silk robe. He got about half of the mummy in the photo and figured that was all he needed.

The antique dealer probably wouldn't want the mummy, but maybe he could find someone else who would be willing to pay money for it. Anyway, it made an interesting picture for his collection.

* * *

After showing a few of his photos to Richards the wiry man returned to the cavern to collect those items that Richards had agreed to buy. The money he got for them kept him going . . . for a while.

CHAPTER THIRTY-TWO
Tuesday, May 22, 2007
San Francisco International Airport

Jeremy had insisted upon driving Felica to SFO. She had argued that she and the other members of her archeology team weren't going to be gone that long, that she could always leave her car at the University and catch a ride with Professor Thompson and, finally, that the University would reimburse her for parking fees if she had to leave her car in the long-term parking lot. Jeremy wouldn't listen to any of those arguments. And as he dropped her off at curbside check-in, folded his arms around her and kissed her softly but passionately for a full minute, until the baggage handler's exaggerated throat-clearing separated them, Felicia fully appreciated his chauffeur services.

Felicia waved goodbye as Jeremy drove away to begin his day in his office down in Silicon Valley. With resignation she turned and pushed through the doors behind her to join the multitudes in their endless lines waiting to be scrutinized, remotely searched by machines and to have her baggage pawed over by the minimum wage guardians of the nation. Almost thirty minutes later she finally left behind the admonishments to remove her shoes, put her carry-on belongings in a plastic wash basin that was then delivered up to the almighty x-ray machine and, in the name of all that was Holy, do not dare to carry with her more than three ounces of any liquid except in a plastic bottle inside a see-thru plastic bag. She managed to squeeze back into her shoes, retrieved her very large purse, advertised as being shaped to put minimal strain on your back, slung it over her shoulder and looked for a Departures board in order to see which gate her flight would leave from. Felicia wondered if it would be possible to exchange her airline ticket for a ticket on a cruise ship going to the islands.

Now that she was past security Felica made her way along the concourse and down to the gate for her flight with only minimal jostling from the hordes of people heading the same way she was. She found the correct gate, but got no encouragement there. The sign behind the check-in counter proclaimed that the flight she and the others were supposed to take was delayed. No time given for depature. Felicia made her way back up the concourse and purchased a latte and a bagel with cream cheese for approximately the amount she had put down the last time she bought a new car.

She was turning around to return to the gate when she heard, "Ah, Felicia, prompt as always."

Professor Thompson, wide smile set on his face, small carry-on bag slung over his shoulder, bore down upon her. Three paces behind him Hwang Tam followed, his left hand pulling a wheeled carry-on bag with extendible handle, his right hand thrust out of sight in the side pocket of his sportcoat.

The Professor took the news that their flight was delayed very much in stride.

"Well, looks like I'll have time to join you in a coffee and a bagel. How about you Hwang?"

"Thank you, no, Professor. I think I'll just find a seat and catch up on my reading."

Felica watched Hwang go off ahead of them and waited for the Professor to collect his drink and bagel. That completed she joined the Professor in the walk back down to their gate.

Hwang Tam had picked a seat in a row looking out to the runways. Since there was only one other seat vacant between him and a heavyset man dressed in shorts and an overly loud aloha shirt, Felicia and Professor Thompson had to find seats in another row. From the number of people sitting around in the waiting area Felicia judged the flight to be fairly full. Their flight was scheduled to leave at 9:10 a.m.

* * *

At 11:07 a.m. the signboard behind the check-in counter still only gave the information that their flight was delayed. At 11:09 a.m. a pert and perky airline employee picked up the microphone behind the counter to announce that while their airline was oh-so-sorry it would probably be less than an hour more until they could board. She then fled the area before she could be inundated with passengers' questions.

* * *

Coming back from the bathroom down the long concourse at 12:14 p.m. Felicia heard the announcement that their flight was now boarding. Threading her way between the people whose boarding passes proclaimed that they would be the last allowed on the plane, but who insisted on crowding as closely as possible around the gate, she caught up with Professor Thompson and Hwang Tam. They made their way onboard with Felicia only getting struck in the shins two or three times by overly large carry-on bags.

Their seats were one row back from the exit row seats in the middle of the plane. They had one aisle seat in the center section and two adjoining seats along the side of the plane. Hwang Tam practically vaulted into the window seat while Professor Thompson slid into the aisle seat in the middle section. The seat next to him turned out to be one of the three empty seats on the whole plane. Hwang Tam stored his large rolling carry-on in the overhead bin, taking up almost all the space there. Felicia shoved her bag under the seat in front of her and tried to find room to fit her feet there too.

Felicia looked at her watch. It was approaching 12:30. She breathed deeply. Only a little over five hours to endure sitting next to Hwang Tam. She could handle it.

"Ladies and Gentlemen. I'm sorry to inform you that we have a small problem with one of the cargo hatch doors. We will need to get a mechanic out to fix the door before we can take off. The Captain will let you know as soon as he hears that we are cleared for takeoff."

The voice from the overhead speakers seemed to resonate with doom.

How long, Felicia wondered, *can I put up with sitting next to Hwang Tam? Maybe I could hide in the bathroom for the whole flight?*

CHAPTER THIRTY-THREE

Felicia glanced at her watch for the one hundred and sixty-seventh time since take-off – their long-delayed takeoff. Since takeoff she had stared often at Professor Thompson, sleeping peacefully and comfortably sprawled somewhat over the empty seat next to him. She had also tried, unsuccessfully, to ignore Hwang Tam who insisted on fidgeting, snorting, noisily blowing his nose and continually adjusting the air vent. Half of the time he adjusted Felicia's air vent in error and she had to re-set it herself. He also put his elbow firmly on the center armrest and no gentle nudges from Felicia could get him to relinquish any portion of it. Felicia glanced at her watch for the one hundred and sixth-eighth time since take-off.

Just then the pilot came on the speaker system to announce that they were only thirty minutes out of Kona, that the temperature was eighty-five degrees and that local time 3:30 p.m.

Felicia set about re-setting her watch to local time. She had just completed that action when it struck her. They wouldn't be arriving until 4:00 p.m. She had told Lori that the three of them would be getting in a little after noon. Did Lori know that their flight was delayed? She had said that someone from the hotel would pick them up and deliver them to the Pono Hale. Was the person still waiting for them?

Lori looked back over at Professor Thompson. Should she wake him? Would he blame her if they had to wait at the airport, in the heat?

As she tried to think her eyes lit upon the answer – right in front of her. The air phone set into the back of the seat.

It took less than a minute, aided by the fact that Felicia had memorized her credit card numbers long long ago, for Felicia to dial

Lori's cell phone number, retrieved from a card in her wallet. She held her breath waiting for the call to be answered.

CHAPTER THIRTY-FOUR

The buzz from the cell phone in her pants pocket interrupted Lori. She had just discovered that Keoki had returned from the airport without picking up the archeology team from Stanford.

Lori fumbled in her pocket pulling out her phone and flipping it open. Keoki turned to amble away.

"Whoa! Don't walk away Keoki; I'm not done with you. Hello? Oh, hello Felicia. Where are you? How long until you touch down? Okay, my shuttle driver just got back. I'll have him turn around and get back down to the airport to meet you. He should be there by the time you and the others collect your luggage. No . . . no trouble at all. I'll see you up at the Pono Family Hale for dinner tonight. Yes. Yes. Mom's really looking forward to this. She's been getting everything ready for the last two days. Okay, see you later."

Lori folded her phone and put it away just in time to catch Keoki who was still trying to get out of sight. Lori's heels clicked across the tiled floor of the lobby. "Keoki, stop right there!"

Caught, Keoki stopped and looked everywhere but at Lori.

"What the hell are you doing? You heard me tell you – "

"Oh? You was talking to me? I thought you was talking on the phone an' I no want bother you. I didn't know you talk to me."

Lori inhaled in order to explode properly, thought about it and noisily released her breath. It wasn't worth it to get into it with Keoki right now. And she could just hear the shop steward defending Keoki, *Hey, you were on the phone. He said he thought you were talking to someone else. So why get so mad? Really over the line, eh?*

"Forget it. I need you to get back down to the airport. The archeology team coming here had their flight delayed, but they're only about a half hour out now. You should be able to meet them by the time they touch down, disembark and pick up their luggage. Take the shuttle back down there and pick up the three of them."

Keoki ran his hand through his hair, down the back of his head and under the back of his shirt in order to scratch an uku bite between his shoulder blades.

"I don' know, Lori. Been a long day for me what with dat group I had to take for catch da early flight to Honolulu. I mean, I put in a full day already. Maybe somebody else oughta go down an' meet dem?"

"There's nobody else working today who can drive the shuttle. So long day or not, you're it."

"I don' know . . . Overtime is nice, but . . ."

"Who said overtime?"

"Oh, hey, gotta. I start seven thirty this morning."

Lori mentally counted to ten, looked up at the ceiling, took a deep breath and let it out.

"Okay, overtime it is. Now get going."

Keoki just stood there looking expectantly at Lori.

"What?"

"You know, my back killin' me. Gonna be three of dem, huh? I bet heavy bags. Afraid maybe my back go out, an' den nobody for drive dem back."

"What do you want, Keoki?"

"I think maybe send someone with me? Can drive okay, but not so sure about lifting. Maybe someone come with for lift?"

Lori could feel the acid building in her stomach and climbing up her throat. She didn't want to take an antacid in front of Keoki. She looked around the lobby.

"Peter! Peter, come here please."

Peter Sakamoto, dressed in his bartender outfit, changed course as he crossed the lobby and walked over to where Lori and Keoki stood.

"Yes, Lori?"

"Peter, I need you to go with Keoki down to the airport and help pick up three guests."

Peter frowned slightly before responding, "Why me? Why not one of the valets?"

Lori felt frustrated at having to explain things all the time. *Why can't I just get people who will do what they're told without questioning me?*

"Because Michael is off today, on vacation, and Jerry called in sick. We only have Frances handling all the valet duties."

Lori squared her shoulders, willed the bile rising in her throat back down to her stomach, and spoke more forcefully than she meant to.

"So if that answers your questions, Peter, and if you're *happy* now, Keoki, I want to see the two of you in that shuttle and on your way down to the airport . . . and in the next thirty seconds!"

Keoki figured that he'd gotten all he could. Peter was actually pleased that he could sit down for a good part of his shift. His partner, Ambrocio, would bitch like heck when he got back, but nothing new about that.

The two men looked at each other, Keoki gave a jerk of his head and they headed out to the curb where Keoki had parked the shuttle van.

As they climbed in and Keoki turned the key in the ignition he opened his mouth to brag to Peter about the overtime pay he'd talked Lori into. Then Keoki shut his mouth, thinking that Peter might claim part of that money if he knew about it. He'd at least go to Lori asking for the same deal, and then she might go back on her word. Especially if she did a strict accounting of Keoki's hours. No, best to keep his mouth shut . . . and the deal with Lori to himself.

* * *

Keoki pulled the shuttle in at the Waikoloa, drove down by the King's Shops and filled up the tank with gas. The hotel had an arrangement there with the mini-serve station. He signed the receipt so that the station could bill the hotel, pocketed the five dollar bill the girl behind the counter slipped him in exchange for the extra five gallons of gas that she would bill the hotel for but that had not gone into the van's tank. Keoki tried to stroke the girl's cheek but she pulled back too quickly for him. He shrugged, climbed back in the van and he and Peter continued on their run to the airport.

* * *

Once back on the road Keoki reached under the driver's seat and pulled out a can of beer from a brown paper bag. He popped the top while steadying the steering wheel with his left knee. A maneuver that gave Peter some anxious moments. Driving now with his right hand Keoki took a gulp of his beer and then rested his left elbow on the windowsill beside him.

"Hey, Keoki, gimme sip?"

"Sorry, brah, only got da one today." Keoki didn't mention that he had earlier consumed the five other beers from the six-pack that he had hidden on the shuttle when he picked it up this morning. Now there was only this one beer left, and he wasn't about to share it.

Grumbling to himself Peter slumped against the door on his side. Suddenly he began searching through his pockets, and he brightened up considerably when he located the object of his search – a half-smoked marijuana cigarette.

Peter carefully lit the roach and inhaled deeply. A look of peaceful satisfaction settled over his face.

Keoki took another sip of his beer.

"Hey, Peter, brah. How's about give me one hit?"

Peter smiled blissfully at Keoki. He didn't even care that most of Keoki's attention was focused on him rather than on the road.

"Sorry, brah . . . only got da one today," and Peter took another hit. When he blew out the smoke he made a point of blowing it out the window and not toward Keoki.

Payback's a bitch, huh! Peter thought.

CHAPTER THIRTY-FIVE

Felicia, Professor Thompson and Hwang Tam all retrieved their luggage from the baggage carousel, carried it over by the curb and then took seats in the shade by the planter.

After waiting for thirty minutes Professor Thompson announced his intention to get a rental car.

"You two wait here for the hotel shuttle," he decreed standing up and massaging his neck. "I'm going to get a rental car so that we have some alternate transportation should we need it."

Felicia stood up, "Are you sure you don't want me to come with you, Professor?"

"No, no . . . you and Hwang stay here. I won't be long."

Felicia groaned inwardly as she watched the Professor walk across the road and board one of the rental car shuttles.

* * *

"You'll soon be rid of me."

Felicia jerked back from her private thoughts as she realized Hwang Tam had spoken to her.

"Excuse me?"

"I said, 'you'll soon be rid of me'. My year at Stanford will soon end and I will return to the University of Beijing. And I expect you will be just as pleased with that as I will be. After all, we have not had an exactly cordial relationship."

"I have been nothing but polite to you."

"Oh, yes. Extremely polite. As I would be polite to a maid or a waiter." Hwang Tam swiveled to face Felicia. "You have been resentful of me ever since I arrived at the Archeology Department at Stanford."

"That's not true!"

"It is. You have been resentful of me . . . and afraid of me."

"Afraid? Why would I be afraid of you?"

"You are afraid of anyone who might displace you. You have feared that I would become Professor Thompson's favorite and that if you lost his favor . . . " Hwang Tam let his words dangle there in the air to be completed in Felicia's mind.

Felicia and Hwang Tam were concentrating so furiously on each other that neither of them noticed the Queen's Beach Hotel Shuttle pull up at the curb opposite them.

* * *

Keoki came around from the driver's side of the shuttle and approached the haole wahine sitting on the concrete bench next to a pake in a suit and tie.

"Hey, howzit folks? You going Queen's Beach Hotel?"

Felicia stood up and addressed the driver of the shuttle, "Actually we're going to the Pono Family Hale. And . . . oh, I think I remember you. You're Keoki, right? You drove us when I was over here last time."

Keoki ducked his head to one side and looked more carefully at the wahine.

"Oooh, yeah! Right. You da girlfren of Haunani's son, right? Yeah, yeah, I drive you las' time you here. Oh, yeah, for da funeral. Sad time." Keoki gave a deep sigh to show how touched he had been by the funeral. Then he brightened up. "But not here for funeral now. So, dis all you luggage? We thought was three of you."

"There are three of us," Hwang Tam said. He stood also and stepped to the side of his luggage. "Professor Thompson went to see about a rental car – since you were not here when we arrived."

CHAPTER THIRTY-SIX

Keoki stood there, a broad smile on his face while pictures of the Chinese tourist lying flat on his back on the ground with his face broken and bloodied flitted through his mind. *Screw you, asshole. But you ain't worth my job.*

"Oh, sorry, had to stop an' fill up with gas up Waikoloa. Okay now, let's get da bags in da shuttle, Peter." Keoki almost forgot and started to reach for one of Felicia's bags, then he caught himself. He was the driver . . . Peter was along to handle the bags. Keoki stepped around to the back of the van and opened the door for Peter.

"Hey, Keoki," Peter hissed, "some kine jerk, eh?"

Keoki nodded but kept his smile plastered on his face as he looked over Peter's back toward Hwang Tam and Felicia.

Peter had just finished loading the last of the bags, which included the Professor's luggage, when the beep of a car horn made him jump.

"Sorry about that," Professor Thompson said as he climbed out of the white subcompact Chevy Aveo that he had rented.

Rubbing his hands together Professor Thompson stepped briskly over to the small group.

"Well, I see our transportation has arrived. And I assume all the luggage has been loaded. Nothing left then but to proceed to our lodgings."

"Shall I ride with you, Professor?" Felicia asked eagerly.

"Ooh, no need to squeeze anyone else into this little car. I think the air conditioning is less than adequate anyway. No, Felicia, you and Hwang Tam can have a little more room to yourselves by going in the hotel shuttle." The Professor did not add out loud, but he thought *And I won't have to listen to the two of you snipe at each other.*

Professor Thompson turned to Keoki and Peter who were standing waiting for the small group to sort itself out.

"I'll follow you. Please make sure that you don't lose me."

"No problem, sir," Keoki replied, "I go slow an' can always pull over an' wait for you if you no can keep up."

"Excellent," the Professor said as he turned back to his rental car, "let's be on our way then."

Peter stepped over to the front door of the shuttle in order to help Felicia in. Hwang Tam quickly climbed in ahead of Felicia and took an aisle seat in the first row behind the driver. Felicia clamped her mouth shut and allowed Peter to help her up the steps into the shuttle. She settled in two rows behind Hwang Tam, on the opposite side of the aisle and next to a window.

Peter and Keoki exchanged glances, then Keoki climbed up and sat down in the drivers' seat while Peter took the aisle seat across from Hwang Tam. Keoki pulled the lever that closed the door and pulled slowly away from the curb. Professor Thompson turned the air conditioner up a notch and followed behind. He began humming a hapa-haole song from when he had been here years before – *My Little Grass Shack.*

CHAPTER THIRTY-SEVEN

Keoki's normal tourist patter, *On a good day you can see da observatories on top Mauna Kea . . . Da lava flows you see here from a long time ago . . . People gather da white rocks an' den leave messages . . . Hawai`i da biggest island an' farthest south*, all fell flat when directed at Hwang Tam. Peter didn't even try. He was out of his element without a bar, bottles and glasses between him and this tourist.

Keoki tried another tack, "So," he said glancing briefly back over his shoulder at Hwang Tam, "why you come Hawai`i?"

A sour expression crossed Hwang Tam's face, but he replied, "We're here to inspect some bones for the hotel. Fortunately I only have to be here until the end of the week. Then I return to China."

Keoki and Peter digested that information.

Interested, Peter asked, "An' why you come United States?"

Hwang Tam leaned back in his seat and spoke so softly that both men had to strain a little in order to hear him.

"I came looking for proof."

"Proof? What kine proof?"

"Proof that would guarantee my future in the Archeology Department at Beijing University," Hwang Tam answered as he looked out the window at the passing lava fields. Keoki started to ask another question but just then Hwang Tam continued, "Proof that my ancestors explored farther than anyone has yet guessed. Proof that the Chinese people reached North America long before the barbarians of the West."

"So, what would be *proof*?"

"Relics, artifacts," seeing the look of incomprehension on both faces, Hwang Tam explained, "things they left behind that could only have belonged to Chinese explorers . . . things of great antiquity . . . great age. Tools, personal items, weapons."

Hwang Tam did not notice how the interest of one of the men perked up at the mention of weapons.

"Things like dat, would be proof?" the man asked.

Hwang Tam nodded.

"An' dey going be worth . . . money?" the other man asked.

"If I could find the proof I'm looking for . . . it would indeed be worth money. Lots of money," Hwang Tam leaned forward in his eagerness, but immediately slumped back again. "But it's hopeless, I leave on Friday and I found nothing definite, nothing of incontrovertible proof on the mainland."

"Ah, but now you in Hawai`i."

The shuttle continued on up the highway toward the Pono Family Hale. Quiet now, each person wrapped in his or her own thoughts.

Felicia stared out her window in the van, oblivious to the men's conversation . . . apprehensive about spending the next few days, and nights, under the microscope of her future mother-in-law.

CHAPTER THIRTY-EIGHT

Keoki wrestled the shuttle through the open gate, across the empty parking lot and up the slight incline to the far end of the parking lot where another gate, closed this time, blocked further access.

"Get da gate," he directed Peter.

Peter shook his head slightly, jumped down from the shuttle, walked over to the gate and unlatched it. He pushed the heavy metal gate, shaped like a triangle with its apex at the end away from the support post, back and held it to keep it from swinging closed while Keoki drove through. He was slightly pissed off, but not at all surprised, when Keoki kept on driving up the packed earth road after clearing the gate. Professor Thompson, following in the little white rental car, tagged along behind the hotel shuttle. He didn't stop for Peter either, but Peter hadn't expected him to stop.

Peter closed the gate, relatched it and set off on foot up the road after the shuttle. He wondered what might happen to Keoki if Lori were to find out he drank while driving the bus. He wondered if he could arrange that.

* * *

Haunani and Teri were waiting underneath the roof of the broad wood-planked lanai of the family house when Keoki pulled up in the shuttle. The lanai looked over the grounds of the family estate that stretched down the hill, and also looked out over the blue ocean toward the setting sun. Haunani was unperturbed at the late arrival of her guests, while Teri had been fretting – worried that something might have happened on the drive up from Kona. The Queen Ka'ahumanu Highway was known for the really bad accidents that happened there frequently. Most were caused by the fact that the police were easy to spot, which encouraged many people, Haunani among them, to exceed the posted speed limit.

Keoki opened the door and exited first in order to assist his passengers as they descended from the shuttle. In the meantime Professor Thompson pulled up and parked behind the shuttle. He stretched his tall lanky frame as he unfolded from the white subcompact rental.

"Aloha, e komo mai!" Haunani called as she descended the steps from the lanai. She went first to Felicia and wrapped her in a welcoming hug. Felicia had felt Haunani's hug when she had last visited, but this time she also felt Haunani stiffen and draw back from her. Haunani still smiled warmly at Felicia, but there was a hint of something hiding behind her smile.

Haunani went on to greet each of her other guests. Professor Thompson hugged her in return while Hwang Tam simply stiffened at her touch and gave her a simple short bow when released.

"Well, welcome to you all. Come in now. Dinner will be ready soon. We can have drinks, sit on the lanai and watch the sun go down. So . . . come in," and with that Haunani beckoned the group to join her in her house.

Peter put one bag under his left arm and picked up two more with his free hands. He looked over at Keoki who was just getting ready to lean back against the shuttle.

"Oh, no, man. Now you help me. Grab da other bags an' let's go."

Keoki started to protest, saw the look in Peter's eyes and decided the last bags weren't that heavy after all.

* * *

Once inside Haunani showed Keoki and Peter which rooms each of the bags went in. Hwang Tam and Professor Thompson were sharing Teri and Frank's old bedroom. Felicia would share a small room with Teri back off the kitchen.

Having put the luggage in the bedrooms, Keoki and Peter returned to the living room to be served iced tea by Haunani.

"Thank you, you boys must be thirsty."

Keoki thought he'd rather have something a little stronger to drink but changed his mind when Professor Thompson joined the two of them and quietly gave them each a ten-dollar bill.

"I appreciate you meeting us at the airport and bringing us all the way up here."

Ten dollars . . . and overtime pay. Not a bad day, thought Keoki.

As the Professor turned and moved back to join the rest of the group Peter whispered into Keoki's ear, "Hey, finish da tea an' let's go. That ten no make up for da tips I lose not being at da bar."

Keoki waved his hand by his ear to shut out Peter's voice. The conversation he heard from across the room was much more interesting.

"Listen," he hissed.

The three members of the archeology team were gathered in front of an eight-foot long Koa wood table. It was formed from a thick slab of wood and supported by legs as big around as a man's thigh. On top of the table a fine old piece of kapa ran the entire length of the table and overhung both ends. Scattered over the kapa were numerous pieces of family memorabilia – sea shells, kukui nut leis and bracelets, three old calabashes of various sizes, an ashtray from the MGM Grand in Reno, photos spanning several decades, three tiny but lucky ceramic frogs, a small lei o mano that resembled nothing less than a set of brass knuckles, except that these knuckles were studded with Tiger shark teeth, and a number of dried leis that had yet to be returned to the land.

But what held the team's attention at the moment was a blue and white porcelain platter. Hwang Tam held it carefully in his left hand and turned it first one way and then the other as he inspected every bit of it.

"Ming Dynasty," he pronounced. "Excellent condition."

"Thank you," said Haunani. "It's been in our family for generations, even since our family lived down by Kona."

"And how did your family acquire it?"

"That I really couldn't say. Our family left the Kona area . . . probably about the time that the Civil War ended. We moved up here for . . . personal family reasons."

"May I see the platter?" Professor Thompson asked.

Reluctantly Hwang Tam let Professor Thompson take the platter from him. The Professor examined the platter much the same as Hwang Tam had done.

"You're correct, Hwang. It is Ming Dynasty, very old, and in excellent condition." He turned and reluctantly passed the platter back to Haunani who returned it to its place on the table. "And very valuable, madame, should you wish to sell it . . . or donate it to a museum," he continued as he rotated and rubbed his neck.

"I thank you both for the information," Haunani said turning back to the group, "but our family heirlooms are just that . . . heirlooms, part of our family's memory and history. Not for sale . . . or for some museum to put on display. Well, I imagine the three of you are hungry after your long flight, shall we sit down to dinner now?"

Taking Haunani's words as their clue, Peter and Keoki excused themselves and drove back down to the hotel in the shuttle van.

* * *

As the sun settled itself down to sleep far out over the edge of the ocean, Haunani went around turning on several lamps which cast a soft light throughout the room.

Hwang Tam was the last to take his place at the table for dinner. He looked back several times at the blue and white Ming platter. His mind was a jumble of thoughts, *That platter belongs to China . . . it should be returned . . . if only the old woman could more accurately date its possession by her family.*

Haunani's voice interrupted his thoughts. "Mr. Tam? Why don't you sit here beside me. I'd like to know more about you."

Hwang Tam didn't bother to correct the old Hawai`ian woman. After being away from home for a year he was almost used to ignorant people mixing up his surname and his given name.

CHAPTER THIRTY-NINE

The dining table was arranged for family-style eating and so, after Haunani said the blessing, platters and bowls were passed from one person to another and then back again. It was a good thing that the dining table was even more well-built than the side table with its family memorabilia. Haunani had outdone herself in preparing the welcoming meal for her guests. In addition to the large rice pot the meal included ahi sashimi, potato-mac salad, green salad with papaya seed dressing, lumpia, chicken long rice, kal bi, both limu and tako poke, lomi salmon and her famous oxtail stew – whose full recipe she still would not share with any of her daughters. There were pitchers of iced tea and lemonade along with a large pot of hot green tea set out to accompany the meal. Several platters were still being passed from one end of the table to the other when Lori and Shari arrived.

"Girls, come sit down and join us," Haunani called to her two daughters.

Lori and Shari each hugged Felicia and then found their seats at the table. Haunani made the introductions of these newest family arrivals and, in turn, introduced the two non-family members of the archeological team.

Conversations between various diners soon raised the noise level in the room to a higher but not uncomfortable level. However Haunani did have to raise her voice slightly in order to gain Hwang Tam's attention.

"I asked you, without being unduly nosey I hope, what the problem with your right hand might be," she repeated as Hwang Tam cocked his head toward her.

For a moment it looked like he might not respond, then he gave a brief and barely audible answer.

"A crocodile ate it."

"Pardon me?" Haunani said as conversations dropped off and all attention turned to Hwang Tam.

Hwang Tam looked around the table. Turned back to his plate and took another mouthful of the chicken long rice. When he looked up into the quietude that had settled over the dinner table he saw that everyone was watching him. He realized that he could not avoid a full explanation. He put his fork, which he held in his left hand, down.

"I said . . . *a crocodile ate it.*"

"And how did that come about?" Haunani asked as she removed a piece of extremely tender meat from a short rib with her fork.

Hwang Tam looked up at the ceiling for a minute in order to compose his thoughts. He kept his right hand in the pocket of the jacket that he had worn ever since the team had met at San Francisco International Airport. His only concession to the tropical weather had been to remove his tie.

"As a young boy I was fascinated with everything scientific, especially the field of natural sciences. I knew everything there was to know about dinosaurs and the wild animals of the world. I made my poor mother nervous with my collections of insects and reptiles. Whenever one of my specimens got free she would not rest until it was found and safely locked away."

Hwang Tam paused to drink some of the hot green tea he had chosen to go with his meal.

"This tea is quite acceptable," he said speaking directly to Haunani. He took another sip and returned to his story.

"I do not know if all of you are aware, but in China children who were born disfigured used to be . . . discarded. Parents could not afford to raise any child whose body was imperfect. I believe this practice has been discontinued . . . for the most part. Similarly, anyone who is handicapped is at a distinct disadvantage. Supposedly society has improved, but it is much more difficult for someone with a handicap to succeed in China than it is here. As I said, I was fascinated with science and with animals. So it was only natural that when I had a chance to work as a volunteer at the Beijing Zoo I leapt at the opportunity. It was marvelous work for a young boy of thirteen. I did not mind shoveling animal manure or carrying and distributing heavy bags and buckets of feed. I was working closely with the animals that I loved." At this point Hwang Tam paused again to sip his tea, and to organize his thoughts.

"It was marvelous. Until one terrible day. A keeper asked me to assist him. There was a crocodile enclosure, a large pond with a four-foot high concrete wall around it. In the enclosure we had a sixteen-foot crocodile . . . and he had injured himself. He had managed to gash the side of his body, near the shoulder. The keeper needed to inject him with some antibiotics and sew the wound closed in order to assure that the wound would not become infected. The keeper lured the crocodile out of the large pond and over to the wall that surrounded the enclosure. He threw the crocodile pieces of raw chicken and dangled a whole chicken in front of him on the end of a pole. Once the crocodile was right alongside the wall the keeper shot him with a hypodermic dart containing anesthesia. The crocodile soon lay quietly and the keeper was able to climb into the enclosure, sew up the wound and administer the antibiotics. The keeper then climbed back out. But no sooner was he out of the enclosure than he remembered that the anesthetic dart was still stuck in the crocodile. He told me to retrieve it. I climbed up on the wall but, since I was much shorter at age thirteen than I am now, I was unable to reach far enough to grab the dart. The keeper held my legs and lowered me over the concrete wall until I was able to take hold of the dart. I pulled the dart out . . . and I think that was what woke the crocodile from his drugged sleep. He whipped his head around and grabbed my right hand with the dart in it. The keeper held onto my legs and the crocodile jerked his head away. My hand remained in his mouth. Before anything else could be done the crocodile had returned to the depths of the pond, my hand in his stomach now."

No one touched their food now. All eyes moved from Hwang Tam's face to his right arm. Seeing their focus Hwang Tam sighed and pulled his right arm out of his pocket.

At the end of his right wrist . . . nothing. Only smooth skin with long-healed scars.

Hwang Tam held his truncated right arm up in the air, moved it from side to side and regarded it himself with interest.

"I've quite learned to use my left hand for everything I need. And I can actually use what is left of my right arm for many tasks. The only real difficulty is the pain."

"Pain?" Teri asked.

"Yes, I get terrible pain in my thumb and first finger." Seeing Teri's look of incomprehension Hwang Tam went on, "Phantom pain. Naturally I have no thumb or first finger of that hand, but my nerves don't know that and so they frequently transmit messages of intense pain to my brain. Sometimes the pain is so fierce that I want to smash my hand into the wall. I did that once. The pain didn't go away."

His face once more blank Hwang Tam returned the empty end of his right arm to the right-hand pocket of his sportcoat once more.

"But I've also learned that people look upon my deformity with either pity . . . or disgust. So it is much easier just to keep it out of sight."

"Thank you, Hwang Tam," Haunani said. "I appreciate that your story is a very painful one to tell. I hope you allow people to see that there is more to you than just your missing hand."

Hwang Tam and Haunani looked long at each other before returning to their plates. Slowly the conversation around the table picked up again.

* * *

Because of the lateness of the hour and the fatigue of the archeological team members, after dinner conversation was brief. Lori reminded the team that the hotel shuttle would pick them up shortly after nine a.m. and bring them to the hotel to examine the site where the bones had been found. She and Shari left together.

Teri went off to her room after showing Felicia to the room assigned to her while Haunani pointed out the way to the bathroom to the two men and showed them their room.

While Professor Thompson put his extra clothes into the top drawer of the only dresser in the room, Hwang Tam prepared to hang his shirts and jacket in the closet. The golf bag annoyed him, with its heavy cloth traveling cover that took up, to his mind, too much space in the closet. He wound up taking the golf bag and travel cover out of the closet and stood it in a corner of the room.

The two men were just getting ready to climb into their beds when Haunani knocked at the door.

"Yes?" Professor Thompson answered.

"I have something for you, Professor"

Opening the door the Professor found Haunani standing there holding a small white cloth bag from which faint wisps of steam rose.

"Here," she said, "this is Hawai`ian salt. I heated it. If you put it on the back of your neck as you prepare to sleep it will take away the ache from your stiff neck. Good night, Professor."

* * *

"Mom?"

Haunani paused with her hand on the doorknob of her own room. She turned to see Teri standing halfway out of her own room. Teri held a light cotton robe around her and looked up and down the hall before stepping over to Haunani.

"What is it?"

In a low whisper Teri asked, "It's okay, Felicia's in the bathroom. Mom, I thought I saw you flinch when you hugged Felicia. Why did you do that?"

Haunani licked her lower lip and gazed down at the wooden flooring for a moment before she answered.

"When I hugged her . . . " her voice became even softer.

Teri stepped up and put her hand on her mother's shoulder.

"What? What is it?"

"I could sense it. Felicia is pregnant. Jeremy and Felicia are going to have a child."

CHAPTER FORTY
Wednesday, May 23, 2007

Professor Thompson rolled over, retrieved his watch from the small table beside his bed and squinted at it in the dim light coming in through the thin window coverings. Ten twenty-eight? How did he oversleep by that much? After puzzling over that question for a minute Professor Thompson realized that he had not reset his watch upon arriving in Hawai`i. It was not quite seven-thirty a.m. yet. A gentle knock at the door confirmed that.

"Professor? Hwang Tam? Are you awake yet?"

Professor Thompson sat up and looked over at Hwang Tam's bed. A lump under the covers grunted and pulled them further up.

"Yes. Yes we're awake."

"Oh, good . . . breakfast in about thirty minutes."

Professor Thompson heard soft footsteps walking away from outside their door. He was tempted to lie back and had already slipped down to where he was resting on one elbow. From under his covers Hwang Tam snorted and cleared his throat. Professor Thompson made up his mind, sat back up and swung his legs over the side of the bed. He grabbed a three-quarter-length robe from a hanger in the closet, picked up his toiletries kit and slipped out the door and down to the bathroom.

* * *

Returning to the bedroom less than fifteen minutes later Professor Thompson had to step aside to avoid bumping into Hwang Tam. Hwang Tam had the top sheet of the bed wrapped around him as he shuffled out of the room and made his way to the bathroom.

Professor Thompson dressed quickly, left the bedroom and found his way back to the living room/dining room. He stepped over to the windows and looked out over the hillside below and the flat ocean beyond.

"Beautiful? Yes?"

Professor Thompson started slightly and then turned to greet Haunani. She had entered the room silently on her bare feet. She carried a Koa wood tray on which rested a ceramic pitcher, four mugs, a porcelain creamer and sugar bowl. Several teaspoons and a stack of paper napkins took up the remaining space on the tray.

"Very beautiful, yes. Must be wonderful waking up each morning to this view."

Haunani placed the tray on the center of the dining table, poured steaming Kona coffee into a mug and stepped over to the Professor. She handed him the cup and her gaze followed his out the window.

"It's one of the reasons I never leave the island."

"Hmmm," Professor Thompson replied as he sipped the coffee.

"Do you need sugar or cream?"

"Oh, no, this is just fine."

"Well, breakfast will be ready in just a few minutes. Relax and enjoy one of the best times of the day here," and Haunani went back through the hallway and into the kitchen at the back of the house.

Seconds after Haunani had disappeared into the kitchen, Hwang Tam entered the room. He was dressed much the same as yesterday, tan slacks and light yellow polo shirt with brown loafers, except that he had left his sportcoat in their bedroom. However he still hid his right hand by keeping it in his pants pocket.

"Coffee," Hwang Tam grunted. He stepped over to the table, filled a mug two-thirds of the way with coffee, followed that with a very large amount of cream and topped the whole thing off with four spoonfuls of sugar. He stirred the light tan coffee and drank a quarter of it with one swallow. Hwang Tam's shoulders rose and fell as the coffee coursed through his system bringing him back to life.

"So," Professor Thompson asked already knowing the answer, "did you sleep well?"

"The trip yesterday must have taken more from me than I was aware." Hwang Tam did not bother to ask the Professor how he had slept.

After waiting a full minute the Professor sipped his coffee, cleared his throat and spoke again.

"You have very few days left now. You must be looking forward to your flight home."

"Not really. It has been almost a full year and I have failed to accomplish what I set out to do. I have some evidence that China reached the North American continent first, before Columbus, but nothing conclusive," he focused his gaze on the Professor as he continued, "nothing that someone else could not quibble about. Nothing that will —" Hwang Tam stopped before completing his sentence out loud, but he completed it in his own mind. *Nothing that will gain me the recognition and advancement that I deserve.*

Professor Thompson took a seat at the dining table. He held his mug in both hands, savoring the warmth as well as the aroma of the fresh-brewed coffee.

"Perhaps it's for the best. Remember, you were . . . are . . . here on sabbatical. Had you found something, some physical evidence to validate your theory, some artifact, it still would have been quite some time until . . ." The Professor returned his attention to his coffee.

Hwang Tam looked sharply at Professor Thompson. He sat down across from the professor and placed his mug on the table.

"Until what?"

Professor Thompson regretted moving the conversation in this direction, but he shrugged his shoulders and went on.

"You know the terms of your sabbatical as well as I. Any artifacts, any relics, anything of historical or cultural value that you find while working with us belongs to the University. If you had found something of interest . . . well, it would have become the property of the Archeological Department. We would naturally have wanted to examine any find, authenticate it, and perhaps allow you to receive some of the credit for your find . . . if it turned out to be legitimate. However, you know the speed with which the Department proceeds in these matters. It would be years until the University completed its studies. And the contract you have with the University prevents you from publishing anything . . . anything . . . without prior authorization from the Department . . . and the Department Chair."

Hwang Tam sat, his coffee ignored, and gazed fiercely at Professor Thompson.

The Professor sat back in his chair and sipped his coffee once more.

"Of course that is all irrelevant since you have not found anything of interest pertaining to your theory. So . . . we'll conduct this minor study at the hotel, and then you'll be on your way back to China while I and Felicia return to the University."

"Did I hear my name mentioned?" Felicia asked as she stepped through the doorway and into the room.

Felicia took a seat at the table, keeping an empty chair between herself and Hwang Tam. She poured herself a cup of coffee and looked at the two men. Professor Thompson sat back, relaxed. Hwang Tam sat upright, tension evident in every aspect of his body.

Felicia looked back and forth between the men again, leaned forward and put her elbows on the table as she raised her mug to her lips. Looking out the window at the clouds far out to sea she said, "Looks like we might have a small disturbance brewing."

* * *

Breakfast that morning was somewhat awkward. For the most part Hwang Tam and Professor Thompson spoke only as necessary. Felicia spoke with the Professor, but avoided even looking at Hwang Tam . . . who returned the favor. Haunani and Teri did their utmost to keep the conversation light and succeeded, mostly.

With plates pushed to one side the group discussed the day's upcoming activities.

"So, how do you begin your work and what are you looking for?" Teri asked.

Professor Thompson pulled his pipe out of his pocket, searched for a light and then noticed how closely Haunani was watching him. He put the pipe away, thought for a moment and responded.

"On a more . . . important . . . project we would of course have done much more extensive preparation. Not only of the site itself but also in regard to research of similar investigations. With this project however we can move much more quickly. We will simply excavate the bones in the area, catalogue them and package them for . . . well, for some sort of reburial I suppose. Someplace away from the area that the hotel wishes to use.

Teri looked at Haunani sitting next to her. She noticed the darkening of her skin as the blood crept up to flush first her ears and then her cheeks. Under the table Teri laid her hand on Haunani's and squeezed. Haunani relaxed her shoulders, took a sip of green tea from her mug and addressed Professor Thompson in a carefully modulated voice.

"I and many others like me would stipulate that this is actually a very important project. After all, these are our ancestors that you propose to *package*."

Professor Thompson chewed on his lower lip for a moment.

"Of course. That was somewhat insensitive of me. Certainly we will treat these artifacts with all due respect."

"*With all due respect*, Professor, we prefer the term iwi. While they are bones, they are cherished and the word iwi itself is found in many expressions referring to life and old age among other things. So, yes, we certainly hope that you . . . and your team . . . treat our ancestors with all due respect." Haunani pushed back her chair and stood, "Teri, could you give me a hand, please?"

While Teri and Haunani cleared the table, the three members of the archeological team reviewed their plans for the day.

* * *

"I don't really see why you need me in this endeavor. It seems very straightforward and she and you should be able to handle it quite well by yourselves."

"The University sent us over here to work as a team. The University paid for all of us to come over here. We will work together on this project, no matter how small it actually turns out to be," frustrated at not being able to light up his pipe Professor Thompson drank some more coffee, even though he knew it might mean a slight acid attack later on in the day.

Trying to keep the peace he tried another approach.

"This will not take us long. Working together we can finish more quickly and, possibly, even have time to ourselves. Time perhaps for other *personal* investigations."

Hwang Tam was not satisfied, but knew that the Professor would not give more than that. He gave a grunt but nodded his head.

A screeching of tires in the gravel out behind the house announced that Keoki was there to drive them all down to the hotel.

The screen door to the kitchen at the back of the house opened and slammed shut.

"Okay all you folks, shuttle time. Keoki's here fo' take you down to da Queen's Beach Resort Hotel. No pushin' no shovin' plenny room fo' everyone," Keoki's voice rang out from the kitchen. His words were followed by a sound similar to a watermelon being thumped by a shopper in a market.

"Owww! Damn! Owww, stop! Okay, okay Haunani, sorry, I'm sorry! No, I won't do it again. Owww!" This was followed by the sound of the screen door opening and slamming shut again.

* * *

Felica, Professor Thompson and Hwang Tam gathered their things, notebooks and pens and cameras along with sunglasses and hats, and made their way down the hallway, through the kitchen and out to the graveled parking area behind the house. Professor Thompson carried all of his materials in a small daypack. Teri and Haunani made sure the stove was turned off, closed up the house and joined the archeological team members outside.

The Queen's Beach Resort Hotel shuttle sat there waiting for them. Next to the open door, his right hand outstretched and ready to assist them into the vehicle, Keoki stood. With his left hand he rubbed and rubbed the top of his head, his eyes still sparkling with tears of pain.

CHAPTER FORTY-ONE

Perhaps as a result of Haunani's chastisement Keoki drove smoothly and quickly down from the Pono Family Hale to the Queen's Beach Resort Hotel. As they drove along the Queen Ka`ahumanu Highway Teri and Felicia, sitting together in the back of the shuttle, gazed out over the sea.

"So beautiful," Felicia said. "The sunlight looks like diamonds sparkling on the waves."

"Yes," Teri agreed. She wondered if she should bring up the subject of the baby that Haunani had said Felicia was carrying. She wondered if Felicia even knew herself that she was pregnant. Teri knew that her mother had a gift. After all, she had told Teri that Sean and Megan were expecting a child even though they were on the mainland while Haunani was on the island. Teri often wondered what other things her mother knew but did not share with her. She guessed that her mother knew how much Teri missed Frank, but she wondered if her mother also knew how that pain was becoming a little less each day.

Two rows further up in the shuttle Haunani, sitting by herself, turned around and smiled at Teri and Felicia.

* * *

A few miles down the road from the Pono Family Hale a discreet sign prompted guests arriving at the Queen's Beach Resort Hotel to turn off the Queen Ka`ahumanu highway. Keoki, however, didn't need the sign to tell him when to turn. He also felt that he didn't need the attendant at the security gate to check him and his shuttle in. But he slowed, almost paused, and smiled anyway as he inched the shuttle forward. Curtis, the attendant working the gate at this time, wondered to himself if Keoki had enough attitude to let the shuttle hit the gate if it didn't raise quickly enough. Knowing that he would share in the blame for the broken gate, Curtis hit the button to lift it out of the way just in time to escape being hit by the shuttle's front bumper.

After passing through the security gate the passengers on the shuttle were treated to the beauty of the winding entrance road. This entrance road was bordered by purple bougainvillea on one side and neatly trimmed golf course fairways on the other. Mynah birds hopped here and there along the manicured grass on the side of the road. They seemed always to be looking for something good to eat. A flock of wild turkeys posed and preened along one curve taking up half of the road. The males were totally oblivious to the shuttle's passage, absorbed as they were in displaying their gorgeous plumage and thick wattles for the benefit of the females. The Professor and Hwang Tam were excited to see a pair of mongeese shoot across the road in front of the shuttle only to disappear under the hedge alongside the road.

At the end of the entrance road a large circular drive fronted the Queen's Beach Resort Hotel. It was from here that one first took in the grandeur that was the hotel.

The Queen's Beach Resort Hotel reclined comfortably here on the north end of the Kohala Coast. Wrapped around her like a comfortable quilt were culture, tradition, respectability – and an air of superiority that came from knowing that even in her advanced years she was still superior to the other hotels that stretched down the coast all the way to the Kona International Airport. The Queen's Beach Resort Hotel, like many of those whom she accommodated, still staunchly upheld the traditions of days gone by. While younger travelers to the island often booked first at the hotels that offered twisting waterslides, waterslides that dropped them into free-form pools, along with a broad range of other exciting family activities, the Queen offered calm and tranquility, coupled with a large helping of refinement and grace. Those who chose the Queen's Beach Resort Hotel tended to return again, and again, and yet again. Over the years they brought with them their children, and their children's children. Over the years she became *their* hotel and was referred to as such.

Inside the paved circle of the driveway a thick green lawn surrounded a fourteen-foot tall statue of Queen Ka`ahumanu, the favorite wife of King Kamehameha as well as the woman responsible for breaking the system of kapu in the islands. Queen Ka`ahumanu's statue welcomed guests, both new and returning, to the hotel and to the beautiful Kohala Coast that she and her husband King Kamehameha had so loved. Her statue radiated grace and nobility. Behind the statue the hotel reflected those same qualities. It was largely through the Queen's efforts that the old religion, and the priests of the old religion, had been overthrown. Under the old system of kapu, many people had died for such seemingly trivial and inadvertent acts as letting their shadow fall upon a member of the royalty. Indeed, some of the current employees of the hotel might have had their lineage snapped were it not for the efforts of Queen Ka`ahumanu.

Off to one side of the circular drive, sheltering the valet station, stood an ancient banyan tree. It took extraordinary efforts by the groundskeeping staff to restrain the banyan tree in its quest to take over the hotel.

On exiting the shuttle the archeological team members were greeted as all guests were and given fresh plumeria lei to wear. Only Hwang Tam seemed less than pleased with this welcoming gesture.

* * *

Led by Haunani and Teri the group walked on into the main lobby of the hotel. Keoki, having no other current duties, ambled along behind them – not really part of the group, but still close enough to overhear their conversations.

The group paused, once out of the bright morning sunlight, to appreciate the beauty of the lobby. An open-air atrium surrounded by a waist-high railing extended from the lobby down to the shops on the lower floor and up to the guestrooms above. A planted area on the far side of the atrium held tall thin palm trees, the tallest reaching almost to the railing of the walkway on the top floor. Teri shivered as she stared up and up to that thin railing.

On the walls surrounding the lobby hung ancient Hawai`ian quilts, framed and protected behind thick glass. In each of the corners of the lobby stood statues of long-gone Hawai`ian royalty. Teri pointed out King Kamehameha in one corner and Queen Ka`ahumanu in the opposite corner to the members of the archeological team.

The wall opposite the broad entrance they had come through held a wide opening. Floor to ceiling heavy wooden shutters were pulled back in order to allow the gentle trade winds to enter. The wide opening provided a magnificent view of the broad curve of white sand that was Queen's Beach with the beckoning blue sea beyond. Tiny sparrows flitted here and there throughout the high-ceiling lobby. Hotel guests strolled about taking photos with their top-of-the-line digital cameras.

Off to the left of the group from the Pono Family Hale was the Reception Desk with three young women in matching flowered blouses working behind it.

Lori, dressed in a light green cotton suit with a pale yellow blouse, stepped out from a hallway beside the Reception Desk. Koakane was walking beside her. He wore slippers, bleached jeans and a teeshirt with a Hawai`ian flag on the front. Around his neck he wore a kukui nut lei. Right behind Koakane came two other local men. Koakane saw Keoki at the back of the group and gave a slight lift of his head to acknowledge Keoki's presence.

"Aloha," Lori greeted the group. "Did everyone get a good night's sleep?"

As its leader the Professor assured her that they all had slept well, and that they had greatly enjoyed the breakfast Haunani had prepared for them.

Lori smiled and indicated Koakane with a gesture. She introduced him and his two friends, Brandon and Manu, and explained that they were here today as observers.

"Observers only. They represent . . . native interests in this archeological investigation."

"As long as these *observers* recognize the need to avoid interfering with our investigation there be no problem," Professor Thompson said. "After all, we three are professional archeologists – "

"Vulture culture," Koakane said, just loud enough for all in the group to hear him.

"Pardon me?" Professor Thompson said as he took a step forward.

Koakane also took a step toward the Professor.

"If you haven't heard the phrase before, vulture culture refers to the unfeeling way in which those calling themselves archeologists have desecrated the cultural remains of those they consider less advanced than themselves. Surely you must have heard of those *scientists* who, on the continent, robbed graves in order to collect Indian cultural artifacts and physical remains. Packing those items, including skulls and bones, off to museums to be peered at by hordes of uncaring people."

"I can assure you that is not why we are here. Nor is that current practice in the field of archeology. Which study, by the way, enhances the lives of people today all over the world by helping to understand how cultures arrived at the point they are. We are here simply to determine if the bones –"

"Iwi!"

"If the bones in question are those of native Hawai`ians. And we are here to recover those bones –"

"Iwi!"

"And to deliver them to the appropriate people for . . . whatever disposal is deemed appropriate."

The two men stood facing each other. Between them yawned a dark chasm that it seemed would not be bridged.

Professor Thompson turned away first.

"Well, Ms. Pono, why don't you show us to this investigation area?"

Lori cleared her throat.

"Good idea. If you would all follow me?" and she set out around the corner for the elevators.

Keoki decided to keep his distance from the group and set off another way, down a set of stairs that led past the beachfront bar and along the beach to the proposed tennis court area.

* * *

Just as the group set off behind Lori, Peter came around the corner. He had been checking his supplies at the beachfront bar, which was due to open in another hour. Walking with him was a heavy-set part-Chinese man with a wispy beard and mustache, and shaved head. The man wore the white outfit of a chef but carried his chef's hat in his hand. The two had their heads close together and were keeping their voices low. Peter looked up and recognized Koakane. Koakane glanced at Peter out of the corner of his eye but kept his face blank. Peter paused for a moment and watched intently as the group continued on their way. He bit his lip lightly in thought before turning back to the heavy-set chef.

As the group all squeezed themselves into one elevator, Koakane looked back and watched as Peter and the chef continued on their way across the lobby, their heads once more bent together in secretive conversation.

Koakane frowned.

CHAPTER FORTY-TWO

Lori led her small party out of the elevator, down a corridor and out into the morning sunlight. Sunglasses popped out of pockets and bags and snapped into place somewhat modifying the bright light reflecting off the sand and the water.

Hotel guests lay scattered over the sand like so much debris thrown up by the surf. They eagerly soaked up the rays of the sun, while continually applying sunblock to their delicate skin. In the surf the young children of the hotel guests frolicked, delighting in the miniature waves that attempted to knock them down. Farther out the older progeny of the hotel guests floated on top of the water breathing thru snorkels and viewing the bottom, six feet below them, through diving goggles or masks. Many considered themselves quite brave.

Keoki reached the investigation area before the rest of the group. The yellow *CAUTION – KAPU* tape surrounding the area only kept him out because he thought someone might see him if he ducked under it. As the group approached he casually walked over to examine the small backhoe and tractor that sat off on the far side of the abandoned excavation. He perched on the tractor treads.

* * *

"So, this is our area of interest?" Professor Thompson asked rhetorically. He noted that the area was approximately one hundred and twenty feet in length and maybe seventy feet in width. The excavation was ragged and ran from about six feet deep at the far end to about two feet deep at the hotel end. An access ramp had been cut into the earth at the hotel end in order to allow the backhoe and tractor to get in to work. The Professor noted a small number of bones that had been placed on an old beach towel on this side, the ocean side, of the excavation. He knelt down to examine them briefly.

"Where did you find these bones?" he asked Lori.

"Toward the middle. The backhoe turned up a few bones and the contractor stopped work. He and his men retrieved the bones you see by hand. Then he notified me and, after consultation, we decided to call you and your colleagues in."

"Hmmm," the Professor rubbed his chin in thought.

"Hey, sis, sorry I'm late."

Teri recognized the voice and turned, along with the others, to see Shari making her way over the sand toward them. Shari was carrying her shoes, four-inch heels, in one hand, and waving the other hand in the air to help keep her balance. The soft sand under her feet caused her well-shaped okole to swing seductively from side to side. Everyone could see that she needed assistance in walking across the sand. Everyone but Haunani, Teri and Lori who knew that from the time she could first walk Shari had lived down at the beach – playing in the sand, running in the sand . . . and laying down on a blanket on the sand in the moonlight with one boy after another. Teri shook her head as Shari joined the group.

"So, what have I missed?" she asked grasping Koakane's bicep in order to steady herself as she leaned over the caution tape and peered at the site.

Shari was wearing a halter top under a gauze blouse whose ends were tied just below the halter-top. She had on a pair of low-cut Capri pants and when she bent over the caution tape barrier most of a tattoo, a floral design it appeared, was revealed. Any man whose blood still coursed through his veins would be very interested in seeing how far that tattoo extended.

Haunani, standing next to Teri, whispered in her ear, "What's that?"

"Come on, Mom," Teri whispered back, "you've seen tattoos before."

"Yes, but never one on Shari . . . not there anyway."

Putting her hand up to her mouth to conceal her words even further Teri explained, "They call it a tramp stamp nowadays. Pretty appropriate, I think."

Teri noticed that Koakane, standing right beside Shari, had an excellent view of the tramp stamp . . . and seemed quite interested in it. For some reason that bothered Teri.

Moving away from her mother Teri came around to Koakane's other side. She was paying no attention to what Professor Thompson was saying about the excavation site. Teri moved in close to Koakane, looked over the site and pointed toward the middle.

"Are those more bones over there?" she asked. As she spoke Teri leaned in and across Koakane slightly. Her breast under the thin dark blue silk blouse she was wearing pressed up against the back of his upper arm. He didn't move, and neither did she. She felt her nipple becoming firmer as she stayed in contact with him. Then, flushing a little, she pulled back. Koakane turned and looked in her eyes. Teri turned her head away as the blood rushed to her cheeks.

* * *

"All right," Professor Thompson announced, "our team will spend the rest of today on site looking over the area. From our initial observation we will decide how and where it will be best to proceed tomorrow." He turned to Lori, "I don't expect this to take more than one or two days. Ms. Pono?"

"Yes?"

"If you could get some tables, maybe three or four, eight-foot long tables, and put them along that edge," he indicated the far side of the excavation, "then we'll have a place to lay out our finds."

Professor Thompson shifted the small daypack on his shoulder to a more comfortable position before continuing.

"I think that should do it for now." He looked at his watch. "By the time we finish here it should be time for lunch . . ." He let his words trail off in search of someone to finish his sentence.

"Oh, well Professor, you must have lunch here. The hotel will be happy to accommodate you."

"Thank you, Ms. Pono. Shall we meet you in the lobby in," he looked at his watch again, "say in an hour?"

"I'll see you then Professor."

Teri, Haunani and Lori set off back to the hotel.

Koakane, Brandon and Manu conversed briefly before setting out together across the lawn and toward the area where they had parked their cars.

Shari watched the two groups as they departed. She looked around and found no one interested in her. Shrugging her shoulders she set off after her mother and sisters. Shari made her way through the sand much more easily now.

"Hey, wait up," she called after them.

Keoki started to head off after Koakane and the others. Took a few steps, changed his mind and began walking slowly back to the hotel.

Professor Thompson, Felicia and Hwang Tam ducked under the caution tape, walked down the access ramp at the hotel end of the excavation and began poking about in the earth. As if guided, Professor Thompson moved to an area just past the center of the excavation, dropped down on his knees and, pulling a brush and a small scraper from his daypack, began removing the earth there. He hadn't gone far when his scraper met resistance. He dug more carefully and soon his efforts revealed a skull – a small skull, a child's skull. As he brushed more dirt away he saw that the skull was perfectly formed. The eye sockets were not broken. The cranium was intact. The teeth were still firmly in the jawbone. Looking over his shoulder he shifted position so as to block out Felicia and Hwang Tam's view of him. He gently rocked the skull out of the ground, and then brushed the dirt back into the depression. Looking back he was pleased to see Hwang Tam examining the bones on the beach towel and Felicia removing earth from around what appeared to be a femur. Reaching behind him Professor Thompson slid his daypack around and placed it between his knees. After another quick glance he pulled his handkerchief from his back pocket, wrapped it around the skull and slipped his acquisition into his daypack. Taking a deep breath the Professor returned to digging . . . in another location.

* * *

Some fifty minutes later the Professor decided that they had put in enough time at the site this morning. He got up off his knees, brushed the dirt from his pants and checked his watch once more.

"Well, we better head back to the hotel if we want to have lunch," he proclaimed as he climbed back out of the excavation.

Reluctantly Felicia left off her efforts to unearth a pelvic bone she had located close to the femur. Hwang Tam brought a handful of bones that he had unearthed over to the beach towel, added them to the collection there, slapped his hands together to knock the dirt off them and joined the other two.

"Yes, let's get out of this sun. I would like some ice tea."

As they headed across the sand for the hotel two members of the hotel's maintenance crew approached the dig in an electric cart. They carried folding tables to set up beside the excavation.

* * *

Lori met the three archeologists in the lobby, showed them to the bathrooms in order to clean up, and escorted them to the Plumeria Room where Haunani and Teri waited for them at a table with a beautiful view of the ocean. Lori was persuaded to join the group for lunch. Professor Thompson placed his daypack on the floor between his feet and made sure that one of his feet was always in contact with the bag.

* * *

As lunch progressed Felicia decided that Professor Thompson was in an unusually good mood. She thought perhaps it was the wine. He regaled the table with stories of archeological digs in countries around the world . . . including the last dig of the old outhouse behind the defunct brothel in Nevada City.

"I have to tell you, I've heard people described as being green . . . but Felicia here actually was, well almost the shade of your outfit Ms. Pono."

Felicia flushed but managed a small smile at the memory, while everyone else at the table, including Hwang Tam, laughed loudly.

"Well," said Professor Thompson as he placed his empty wine glass back down on the table, "that was an excellent meal and we are all grateful to you for your hospitality Ms. Pono. I guess we better get back to the excavation and earn our keep."

Following the Professor's example they all pushed back their chairs from the table and began moving slowly toward the door to the restaurant. Once outside the restaurant Haunani and Teri said goodbye and headed back up to the lobby to find Keoki and the shuttle for their return trip to the Pono Family Hale. Lori excused herself and walked away checking her cell phone for messages. Felicia went to the ladies' room while Hwang Tam and the Professor visited the men's room. They all met back down at the excavation shortly afterward.

Koakane, Brandon and Manu were waiting for them. The three members of Malama Pono O Ka 'Āina were sitting on the grass under the palm trees eating plate lunches they had purchased up at the little town of Kawaihae. They continued their duties as observers while the archeologists returned to the excavation.

* * *

By four o'clock Felicia had unearthed not only the femur and pelvic bone but also a tibia, several rib bones and a skull that Professor Thompson declared was that of a male, probably in his early thirties.

Hwang Tam had contributed very little, his digging efforts being interrupted by frequent trips ostensibly to the men's bathroom back at the hotel but in reality just far enough away from the excavation site that the Professor could not see him sitting on a bench and smoking.

On the last of those *bathroom* trips as he sat peacefully smoking a man sat down beside him. One of the locals who had helped transport the archeological team from the airport to the Pono Family Hale. Hwang Tam glanced at the man and returned his concentration to the pleasures of his cigarette.

"You like da plate?"

"What? What plate are you talking about?"

"Da plate up Pono Family Hale. I hear you ask Haunani 'bout it. You like da plate, right?"

"You mean the Ming Dynasty platter that the family has? Yes, it's a very nice platter. Unfortunately I doubt that the family will part with it." Hwang Tam took a long drag on his cigarette. He checked the watch on his left wrist. Almost time to be getting back to the others.

"I know where's another. Same as dat one. I can show you."

Hwang Tam was interested. It might not be definite proof, but if he could determine the provenance of the platter, then along with the sea anchor and the chart he might be able to build up a body of circumstantial evidence large enough to be convincing.

"Where is this platter?"

"I can take you tomorrow. Down Kona side. Only cost you . . . fifty dollars . . . for my services."

Hwang Tam thought for a minute.

"All right, but you only get paid if it is genuine."

The man gave a wide grin.

"No problem. Is *genuine*. After you get here tomorrow morning you take bathroom break, like today. I meet you here an' drive you Kona. Oh, da guy wit' da plate . . . he only take cash, so bring plenny money for him . . . an' no forget da fifty fo' me."

With that the local man got up and headed back up to the hotel. He had a phone call to make.

Hwang Tam wondered if he was being set up for a robbery. But it was worth a chance if he could find a Ming Dynasty platter on this island and could verify that it had been brought here quite long ago. He wouldn't need to pay for it if it didn't meet his expectations.

Stubbing out his cigarette Hwang Tam sauntered back down to the excavation just in time to hear Professor Thompson announce that they were finished for the day.

CHAPTER FORTY-THREE

Haunani met the three archeologists when they arrived back at the Pono Family Hale. She informed them that it would be at least two hours until dinner and thus they had plenty of time to refresh themselves with a shower and or a nap.

Hwang Tam and Felicia came out of their rooms at the same time, each wearing a robe and carrying a bath towel, but Hwang Tam moved faster and shut the door to the bathroom in Felicia's face. She stood there until she heard the water in the shower begin running.

Thoroughly angered all Felicia could think of to do was to complain to Professor Thompson once more. She stomped down the hall to the room that the Professor and Hwang Tam shared, knocked on the door and entered immediately without waiting for a response.

Alone in his room the Professor had thought it safe to examine his newest prize. Imagine his surprise as he sat on his bed turning the skull over and over in his hands when suddenly Felicia burst in on him.

"Professor! Hwang Tam is the most obnoxious irritating rude –" she stopped, mouth open, as she saw the object in the Professor's hands.

"What is –" as Felicia began to speak again the Professor swiftly rose from the bed, crossed over to the door and shut it behind her.

"Quiet, please! There's no point in involving the others."

"But . . . Professor . . . that skull . . . is it . . . it's from the excavation! You found it today? But, why did you bring it back here. Surely you don't intend to keep it?"

The Professor moved back toward the bed but did not sit down.

"This is a magnificent specimen. Much too nice to simply put back into the ground. The University will appreciate having such an item added to its collection."

Felicia's mind spun. She visualized the contents of Professor Thompson's office back at the University. She especially remembered the mokomokai that he was so proud of.

"You don't intend to give that skull to the University. You intend to add it to your private collection in your office. And you snuck it out so that those Hawai`ians overseeing our work wouldn't stop you. Because you know that they would never agree to allow you to take it back to the mainland. Not even if you did donate it to the University. It's one of their ancestors, Professor. They've already told you how they feel about putting their ancestors' bones in a museum."

Professor Thompson cocked his head to one side and blew out a disparaging breath.

"You are so new to this field! You understand so little. When you have worked with indigenous peoples for as long as I have . . . You will see how –"

"I see *now*, Professor. You need to put that skull back. We're here representing the University. If it were found that we'd removed some of the remains we were trusted to identify, the University's reputation would be seriously damaged."

"I don't think– "

"No, you didn't think. You must put that skull back."

Professor Thompson held the skull in his left hand tucked back into his armpit. He raised his right hand, index finger pointing aloft in a gesture he was fond of using in lecture classes.

"I *must* do nothing of the kind. I lead this investigation and I decide– "

"If you don't put that skull back tomorrow . . . I'll tell the leader of the Hawai`ian group overseeing our work."

The Professor's mouth opened and closed without him uttering a word. He looked at Felicia. Her mouth was set in a firm line. Her shoulders were squared and pulled back. There was no flexibility in her bearing.

"Very well. I will return the skull tomorrow," and, turning, the Professor pulled his daypack from under his bed, knelt and repacked the skull. He rose and turned back to Felicia.

Felica nodded once before turning, grasped the doorknob and went to see if Hwang Tam was finished in the bathroom yet.

He wasn't. And when Felicia finally got in there was only enough hot water for a brief shower and rinse.

CHAPTER FORTY-FOUR
Thursday, May 24, 2007

After breakfast that morning Professor Thompson brusquely informed Felicia and Hwang Tam that he needed to make some notes on their work of the previous day.

"We will leave for the excavation site once I've completed my notes. I have already informed Ms. Pono from the hotel as well as Haunani that we will not require the shuttle today. All three of us can fit quite easily into my rental car. That way we can not only go down to the site when I see fit, but we can also return here whenever we are finished for the day."

The Professor went back to his room and his writing. Hwang Tam decided to take a walk. Felicia hung about by the dining table for a while, and then decided to see what Haunani and Teri were doing.

* * *

She found them in the kitchen finishing up the breakfast dishes.

"Can I help?"

"Sure," Teri said, and tossed Felicia a dishtowel.

So while Haunani washed, Teri and Felicia dried. Felicia rubbed furiously at the plates getting them perfectly free of moisture.

"If you rub any harder the color's going to come off that plate," Teri said.

"Sorry, I guess I'm just taking some frustrations out on the china."

"Hwang Tam?" Haunani guessed.

"Him too," Felicia answered. Seeing both women put aside their work and stand looking at her expectantly, Felicia shrugged and continued.

"I guess I just have been expecting too much of other people."

"Jeremy? I swear, if that brother of mine has . . . has . . . well, if he has I'll knock his block off!"

Felicia laughed. "Jeremy? No, he is so sweet. I really feel he cares about me . . . more than anyone else ever has."

"That's a relief, considering . . ."

"What? Considering what, Teri?"

"Oh, the girl's just talking. We're just both so happy you and Jeremy found each other," Haunani put in, and she stepped forward to give Felicia a warm hug.

"Me too, Haunani. Me too."

The three of them went back to finishing up the dishes.

* * *

Professor Thompson came out of the bedroom at 9:30 sharp. Felicia was relieved to see that he was carrying his daypack. He announced that his team was going back down to the hotel to work, assured Haunani and Teri that they needn't accompany the team and went outside to bellow for Hwang Tam when he found out he wasn't in the house.

Hwang Tam strolled back up from his tour of the gardens, proclaimed himself ready to go and joined the Professor and Felicia in the subcompact rental car. Together they drove back down to the hotel.

CHAPTER FORTY-FIVE

Professor Thompson was pleased to discover that the Hawai'ian team of observers from Malama Pono O Ka 'Ãina was nowhere around when he and his team reached the excavation site. He was doubly pleased when Hwang Tam announced almost immediately that he had to visit the bathroom in the hotel. He was less pleased when Felicia made it a point of watching him take the skull out of his day pack and place it on one of the long folding tables along with the other bones that they had disinterred the previous day.

As Felicia and Professor Thompson returned to their efforts at unearthing the bones in the excavation site, Koakane, accompanied by his two companions, reappeared. Standing in the shade of the palm trees they watched as the two members of the archeological team worked. It seemed to Koakane that today the Professor took less care in removing the bones from the earth than he had the day before. Almost as if he no longer cared about the project and just wanted to get it over with.

* * *

Back toward the hotel Hwang Tam smoked a cigarette as he waited by the bench. Now and then he touched the wad of cash, all the American money that he had left at this point, in his left front pocket. He was getting impatient when the wiry local man appeared from around a bush.

"Okay, we go now. You got money for pay?"

Hwang Tam assured him that he did, though he was cautious enough not to show the money to him. Together they set off for the hotel, dodging around the side and coming out in the employee parking lot. Hwang Tam made a face of disgust at the battered old car that the man told him to get into. He cleared the front passenger seat of some fast food debris and gingerly got in. Hwang Tam breathed a sigh of relief as the man managed to get the car started. His relief turned more toward anxiety as they turned onto the highway and accelerated down the highway at an appalling rate of speed.

Hwang Tam wondered if he what he had gotten himself involved in was truly wise.

* * *

Forty-seven minutes later the two men were searching for a parking space along Ali'i Drive. After three minutes the wiry man gave up his efforts and pulled into a parking lot with a machine that dispensed passes in exchange for money inserted in the machine. Rather than get a parking pass from the machine, Hwang Tam's driver walked around among the cars already parked there until he found one with the window slightly open. Pushing carefully he got the window down far enough that he could slip his arm inside and retrieve the parking pass on the dashboard. Placing the pass on his own dashboard the man led Hwang Tam out of the parking lot and down Ali'i Drive.

* * *

The bell over the door gave a cheery jingle as Hwang Tam and his guide entered the store with the **_Antiques and Collectibles_** sign hung outside. Hwang Tam paused just inside the doorway and looked around in the darkened interior. The store was filled with Hawaiiana. Two canoe paddles were propped against a Koa wood table, several long thin wooden throwing spears were displayed sticking out of a large jar and a feather cape was hung from a far wall.

"Mr. Richards, dis da guy I tell you about."

His guide faded back into the shadows as the store's owner glided forward, a broad sharp smile on his face.

"So, what can I interest you in?"

* * *

Back at the excavation site Professor Thompson stood up to stretch his back muscles. He looked around.

"Now where the hell did that blasted Tam get off to?" he muttered to himself. "I'm going to be so happy to be rid of him."

Mopping her brow Felicia stepped carefully over to stand beside the Professor.

"Thank you for putting the skull back, Professor Thompson. I know that on reflection you'll see it was the right thing to do."

The Professor gave a grunt. Looking at Felicia with cold eyes he said in a low voice, "You know I've been thinking. In my last review of your doctoral thesis draft I don't think I mentioned a few problems. When we get back to the University you and I will have to sit down and review your work to date. I think perhaps there's quite a bit there that needs to be . . . smoothed out. Worked over. Probably will involve a little more research. It may take you a longer than we originally thought . . . but I'm sure you want to do the right thing."

Professor Thompson turned back to the scapula and rib cage that he had unearthed.

Felicia stood there . . . trying to make up her mind whether to cry or scream. She chose instead to form a mental picture of Professor Thompson's head as a mokomokai, an elaborate tattoo covering his face while his teeth grinned whitely from the treated skin of his shrunken head. She gritted her teeth to keep from saying anything further and turned her back on the Professor.

* * *

After taking advantage of Lori's hospitality and having another superb lunch at the Plumeria Restaurant, Felicia and Professor Thompson continued their efforts until four o'clock. At that point the Professor announced to Felicia, and the Hawai`ian native group observers, that they were "done for the day", packed up his equipment and headed back to retrieve his rental car from valet parking.

The Professor gave the valet a single dollar for bringing his car around and, in response to the questioning look that Felicia gave him, said, "Screw Tam. After ducking out on the investigation today, let him find his own way back to the house."

It was a silent and cold ride back to the Pono Family Hale, not entirely due to the air conditioning in the rental car.

CHAPTER FORTY-SIX

Fifteen minutes or so after leaving Kona behind them, Hwang Tam's guide quickly pulled off the road at the entrance to the West Hawai`i Veterans Cemetery. As he turned the motor off Hwang Tam tensed. He assumed that his guide was now going to try to rob him of both the money he had left and the items he had purchased at the antique store. Instead of attacking him the wiry man swiveled around in his seat and pulled an envelope from his back pocket. It was bent from his sitting on it for the whole trip.

"Here," the man said, "I show you dis now."

The wiry man had waited to see what Hwang Tam would do when presented with the items in the antique store. He had thought he would faint when he saw how much money Hwang Tam paid for the porcelain platter, and had to sit down, on a hard black expensive Chinese chair, drawing a stink-eye look from Richards, when he next saw how much money changed hands for the old knife he had taken from the lava bubble chamber. Mentally he had kicked himself over and over again for getting only one hundred dollars from Richards for the platter. After all, going back again to that small dark cavern really creeped him out. He saw how Richards had cheated him, giving him so little for items that he turned around and sold for so much more. Five hundred dollars for the platter? Six hundred for the old knife? How much more might he pay for the items still left in that cavern?

Hwang Tam watched carefully as the man pulled a set of instant camera photographs out of the envelope. Like the envelope, they were bent. The man handed them to Hwang Tam. The first thing Hwang Tam noticed was that whoever took the photographs didn't do a very good job. Then he began to notice items in the dark grainy photographs that looked familiar. There were the two canoe paddles and the feather cape that he had just seen in the antique store. One photo showed a woven basket of some sort. Another revealed a particularly vicious-looking statue, probably a representation of a god. Coming to the last picture Hwang Tam felt his heart stop.

Can it be? Have I finally found it?

"This . . . these items . . . they are all in this cave?"

The man scratched his head, bringing an expression of disgust to Hwang Tam's face as he thought he saw something jump from the man's hair.

"Well, not all dere now. Some I sell to da antique store guy," turning he spat out the open window.

"Which ones are still there?"

"Oh, all dem . . . 'cept da paddles an' da spears . . . an' da feather cape. But da ka'ai, da casket fo' da bones an' da god figure an' da lei o mano, dey all stay da cave."

"What about this?" Hwang Tam asked as he thrust the photo of the mummy dressed in a silk robe in the wiry man's face.

Something clicked in the man's brain as he looked at the photo that he had taken.

"Oh, dat?" he asked casually. "Da knife you buy today? I get from dat guy," the wiry man shivered at the memory of taking the knife from the mummified body, "So, you like dat, huh?"

Hwang Tam pulled back as he realized his mistake. But he couldn't deny it.

"Yes, it's . . . interesting. I'd like to have a closer look at it. If I was interested in buying it, naturally I'd want to see it first."

"No problem, I bring 'em to you up at da Pono Family Hale."

"NO! – I mean, that's not possible. In fact, I am leaving tomorrow. I have to fly back to China. Could we go there now?"

The man looked at his watch and shook his head.

"Sorry, I gotta work tonight." He thought a bit. "What time you flight?"

"One o'clock tomorrow."

"Okay, I no work 'til three tomorrow. I meet you in da morning an' take you to da cave. Den after I take you airport. Okay?"

It was Hwang Tam's turn to do some mental calculations.

"All right. Where shall we meet?"

"You know da airport?" When Hwang Tam nodded, the man continued, "I pick you up dere. Out front by Interisland Flights check-in, just down past United, okay?"

"What time?"

"Gotta do dis early, before anyone else come around dere – I pick you up eight o'clock. An' you bring plenny money. Dis worth more than all wha' you buy today from Richards."

Hwang Tam agreed, even though he knew he had very little cash left.

Having reached an agreement, a very satisfactory one, the man lit a cigarette, started the car and pulled out rapidly into traffic. He responded to the blaring horn from the car that he cut off by sticking his arm out the window, middle finger extended.

It had been a good day, and tomorrow promised to be even better.

CHAPTER FORTY-SEVEN

Professor Thompson parked his rental car out back and left Felicia to get herself out of her side of the car. He vaulted up the steps and opened the door to the kitchen. Finding no one there he went first to his bedroom and put his daypack away. He retraced his steps to the kitchen and passed Felicia as she came through the screen door. She headed straight for her bedroom ignoring the Professor. Rummaging through the refrigerator the Professor found a can of beer. Popping the top he walked down the hallway and out into the combination dining and living room.

"Where the hell have you been?"

Sitting in an overstuffed chair by the windows, his feet up on an old ottoman, Hwang Tam lowered the paper he had been reading.

"Oh, Professor, you're back."

"Damn right I'm back. Now answer my question, where the hell did you get off to?"

"I'm sorry, Professor. My stomach upset me again today. I didn't want to worry you, so I was fortunate in being able to catch the hotel shuttle down to the airport. From there I caught a ride with someone going into Kona and found a doctor who was able to see me. He gave me some pills for my stomach. I feel fine now, but I didn't want to chance coming back to the excavation site and becoming sick again."

Professor Thompson glared at Hwang Tam.

"Bullshit!"

Hwang Tam shrugged his shoulders.

"As you wish Professor." He folded the paper and rose from the chair.

Hesitantly he stepped closer to the Professor.

"I know this is not the best of times, but I . . . I have a favor to ask. You know that tomorrow I must return to China. I wondered if I might borrow your rental car to get down to the airport. In fact, I could do you a favor and return it for you. I would even be willing to give you cash to pay the rental charges with – in return for your loaning it to me. Could we arrange that?"

Hwang Tam looked hopefully at Professor Thompson.

Professor Thompson looked at the beer in his hand and debated throwing it at Hwang Tam.

"So . . . you would like to borrow my car tomorrow in order to get down to the airport?"

"Yes."

"And what time did you plan on leaving?"

"I was going to change my flight . . . so I would need to leave here by . . . oh . . . seven o'clock."

"Hmmm," commented Professor Thompson. He walked away from Hwang Tam and over to the dining table. He took a long, refreshing swallow of his beer before turning back to Hwang Tam who was waiting expectantly.

"No . . . way! No way in hell!"

Hwang Tam straightened up and rocked back on his heels at the vehemence in Professor Thompson's voice.

"Tomorrow *is* your last day working for the University. And I intend to see you work that day. I expect you over at the excavation with Felicia and me. And I expect you to keep working there until I tell you that you're finished. We can check the flights in the morning and verify exactly what time you need to be released."

"But . . . but Professor, I think I may have found –"

"You may have found? Found what? Some other tenuous proof for your ridiculous theory? You know, you should really be glad that you didn't find anything. Remember, you work for the University . . . right up until the time you touch foot in China. And while you work for the University, anything that you might find of interest belongs to the University. So if you did find *proof,* well, I think the

University would just have to take possession of that *proof* in order to check it out. And do you know how long it might take the University to check out your proof? Probably until you were ready to retire over there in China. So, actually, you should be happy you did *not* find any proof while you were over here."

Professor Thompson finished his beer and set the empty can down on the table. He gave a soft belch and a sigh.

"Now, I'll tell you what I will do for you. You work with us tomorrow at the excavation site and when I write up and forward your year's evaluation to Beijing University it will be . . . positive. It won't be glowing, but it will be a positive evaluation. Now, you do me a favor and get out of my sight."

Hwang Tam stood a moment more. Nothing he could think of to say would change the Professor's mind, so he went off to their shared bedroom.

Professor Thompson sat down in the chair vacated by Hwang Tam, picked up the newspaper he had left behind and began to read.

* * *

In the bedroom Hwang Tam sat on his bed and unwrapped his purchases from the antique store. He stroked the Ming Dynasty porcelain platter, admiring its beautiful colors. Setting the platter down he picked up the old sailor's knife. The handle, carved in the shape of a dragon with long beard, was especially nice. The blade, sharpened repeatedly a long time ago, still held a very *very* sharp edge.

* * *

At dinner that night Professor Thompson and Hwang Tam were both unusually quiet. The three women didn't seem to notice as they chatted about family doings. Felicia heard many stories of the Pono family for the first time. As the table was being cleared Haunani suggested that Teri and Felicia accompany her in the morning up to the new Hana Hou bakery in Kawaihae.

"We can pick up fresh malasadas for breakfast. We'll have to go early, before seven, in order to be back in time for breakfast."

Hwang Tam smiled as he listened to the women's plans.

CHAPTER FORTY-EIGHT
Friday, May 25, 2007

Hwang Tam lay in his bed, eyes closed, his breathing slow and steady, ears alert to every sound from inside and outside the house. He heard the soft snoring from the bed next to him. Professor Thompson had come to bed late after having three more beers from the refrigerator in the kitchen.

Outside the bedroom door he could hear the soft footsteps of the three women as they tiptoed around in the still dark house, doing their best not to wake Hwang Tam or the Professor. At last he heard the back door to the kitchen open. It closed so quietly that he wasn't quite sure they had all gone out. Then, from the graveled area in back, he heard the sound of Haunani's car starting up . . . and then the crunching sound it made driving away over the gravel. He waited and counted slowly to one hundred.

Rolling his head slowly to the left Hwang Tam observed the outline of the Professor through the faint light from the moon as it yielded the sky to the early morning sun. The Professor was on his left side, turned away from Hwang Tam and still snoring softly.

Hwang Tam slid the covers back, rolled onto his right side and quietly levered himself up to a sitting position. Keeping his mouth closed while he breathed through his nose Hwang Tam quickly dressed. He left off his shoes in order to move as quietly as possible when he crossed over to the dresser. The Professor had, as usual, put his wallet and keys along with his comb and handkerchief in the top drawer of the dresser. Hwang Tam gently pulled the top drawer open, wrapped his hand around the keys in order to stop them from banging together, slid the drawer back closed and turned around.

Professor Thompson was sitting up in his bed, arms around his knees, watching Hwang Tam. He wore undershorts but no shirt.

"So? What do you think you're doing?"

Hwang Tam stepped away from the dresser and back over to his bed on which his suitcase lay and, next to it, the paper bag that held the knife and the Ming Dynasty platter that he had purchased from the antiques dealer.

"I told you yesterday, Professor, I need to be out of here early. You have no need for the rental car . . . I do. I will charge all costs for the car to my credit card."

Hwang Tam put the car keys down on his bed and opened his suitcase. He took the knife and platter out of their bag and laid them also on the bed while he moved some shirts and a pair of pants aside in order to make room in the suitcase for his purchases.

Professor Thompson stood up.

"What are those?" he asked indicating the platter and the knife.

"Items from this island . . . items that add weight to my hypothesis that the Chinese visited North America, and Hawai`i, long before Columbus or Cook."

Professor Thompson reached down and picked up the platter.

"This is the same platter that Mrs. Pono has out in the front room."

"Yes, it is identical. But this one came from a cavern deep inside the volcano . . . a cavern that holds incontrovertible proof of my theory."

"Hmm," the Professor said as he turned the platter upside down to study its bottom. "And you say that this platter is essential to your theory? Well, it is very old, Ming Dynasty. And if it has been in these islands for hundreds of years . . ."

Professor Thompson looked up into Hwang Tam's face and gave a wry smile.

"Something as important as this really should be studied further. And as you acquired it while on sabbatical with the University . . . well, as I pointed out to you yesterday, anything you discover of importance while under my supervision naturally must go back to the University for investigation. So," Professor Thompson stepped over to the dresser and opened the top drawer, "I shall preserve this for you and make sure that it gets back to the University."

Hwang Tam stood for a moment as if he had been struck physically. Then he took two steps over to stand behind the Professor.

"No! That is mine! It is my proof of my theory. Together with the body – "

"Body? What body?" queried the Professor as he turned around, the platter still firmly in his grip.

"Never mind," Hwang Tam exclaimed his voice rising in anger. "Just give me my platter," and he grasped the other end of the platter.

Hwang Tam pulled but the Professor refused to let go. The result was that both men lost their grips and the platter crashed to the floor, breaking into several pieces.

The two men stood for a moment looking at the remains of the platter.

"Oops, sorry, Hwang," the Professor said with a notable absence of sincerity.

"You bastard! You pompous bastard," and even as he spoke Hwang Tam spun back to his bed, scooped up the sailor's knife and, turning, plunged it into the Professor's stomach.

The Professor's mouth dropped open, his eyes bulged. He staggered over to his bed, tried to sit down but missed the edge of the bed and slumped onto the floor. Blood ran down his side and pooled on the floor. His eyes closed while his breath, such as it was, became very faint.

Hwang Tam's first thought was to retrieve his knife, but he couldn't bring himself to do so. He looked down at the shattered platter, bent down and picked up the pieces, stacking them in one pile on the floor. When he had all the pieces that he could find stacked together he picked them up with his left hand and stood.

These can still bolster my theory. But how less impressive they are now, he thought.

Hwang Tam suddenly had a new thought. Holding the pieces of the platter in the crook of his right hand he used his left hand to open the door to the bedroom. Hearing no one else he rightly assumed that the three women had not yet returned to the house.

Out in the front room Hwang Tam carefully scattered the pieces of the platter on the floor in front of the Koa wood table. Then he picked up the matching Ming Dynasty platter from on top of the table and with that in hand returned to his shared bedroom. Quickly he sat down and put his shoes on.

Standing now by his open suitcase he thought to himself, *As far as anyone will ever know the platter I have came from the cave with the mummified body*

Thinking of the body caused Hwang Tam to realize that he had not made provisions for transporting the body from the cave. He needed something to carry the mummified body in. He looked around the room and saw the golf clubs in the thick canvas carry bag propped in the corner. It took only seconds to empty the bag. He turned to the closet to be sure that he had taken all of his clothes out. That's when he noticed the old shirt on a hanger far back in the closet shadows. Perfect for wrapping up the delicate Ming Dynasty platter.

A few minutes later Hwang Tam emerged from the bedroom pulling his wheeled suitcase that now contained Haunani's platter wrapped in Frank's old shirt. The thick canvas golf carry bag was draped over his shoulder. He didn't bother looking back at Professor Thompson curled up on the floor.

Once out the back door Hwang Tam stowed the suitcase and canvas bag in the trunk of the small rental car. He took a few moments to adjust the seat and mirrors before starting the engine. Putting the car in gear he whipped it around and headed around and down the driveway leading out of the Pono Family Hale.

CHAPTER FORTY-NINE

"Look out!" Teri screamed as the rental car with its lights off sped down the gravel driveway past Haunani's car. Haunani was forced halfway off the road, recovered and continued on up to the parking area behind the kitchen.

"Who was that driving?" Teri asked.

"I think it was Hwang Tam," Felicia answered from the back seat.

"But I thought Professor Thompson rented the car."

"He did. And I didn't think he would let Hwang use it."

Screeching to a stop Haunani threw her door open and headed for the back steps leading up to the kitchen. She left the keys in the ignition and the driver's side door open. The other two women rushed after her.

"Professor Thompson?" Haunani called out.

Hearing no response the women made their way down the hall and stopped outside the door to the bedroom that the Professor shared with Hwang Tam. Teri knocked . . . and, getting no response, pushed the door open and flicked on the light switch.

"Oh, God!" Felicia exclaimed.

Haunani rushed over and knelt beside the Professor. She placed her first two fingers under his jaw. "Shhh," she commanded.

The seconds thudded past like coconuts falling from a palm before she looked up at the other two women.

"There's a pulse, but very weak. Felicia, go call 9-1-1 . . . tell them we need an ambulance . . . and the police."

"Should we pull out that knife?" Felicia asked.

"No, that could do more damage, maybe kill him. Now quick, go make that call."

Felicia rushed out of the bedroom.

Teri stood looking around the room. She saw the open dresser. She saw all the blood on the floor. And she saw Frank's golf clubs and golf bag tossed on the floor by the closet opposite Hwang Tam's bed. She stepped over and tried to figure out why the clubs were on the floor. Then she saw the open door to the closet . . . and the empty hanger far back in the closet.

"He took his shirt!"

"What?" Haunani said from her position kneeling beside Professor Thompson.

"Hwang Tam! He took Frank's shirt!"

Haunani tried to understand Teri's concern, but failed.

Felicia rushed back down the corridor and stopped in the doorway.

"The ambulance and the police are both on their way. They wanted to know how he was . . . I said he was pretty bad, oh, and Haunani, your platter is broken. That Ming Dynasty platter is smashed on the floor by the table."

"I need to find him," Teri announced as she pushed past Felicia and out the door.

"Teri! Teri, where are you going," Haunani called after her.

When she got no response from Teri, Haunani looked at Felicia.

"Go! Follow her. Stay with her. Don't let her do anything foolish."

When Felicia didn't move Haunani repeated herself, "Go! Now! Stay with her!" Haunani turned back to Professor Thompson, but could find nothing to do for him.

* * *

Felicia caught up with Teri just as Teri was pulling the driver's door shut and turning the key to start the engine.

"Wait! Where are you going?"

"I've got to catch him," Teri said as the put the car in reverse and started to back up.

"Wait! I'm going with you."

"No, you don't need to."

"Haunani said I had to."

Teri put her foot on the brake, debated with herself for a split second and barked, "Okay then, get in."

She was barreling down the gravel drive before Felicia could get her door fully closed or buckle up her safety harness.

* * *

Teri didn't stop, though she did slow down a little, before pulling out onto the highway. She was doing seventy miles an hour by the time Felicia finished settling into the passenger seat.

"Why are we going after him?"

"He took Frank's shirt."

For a moment Felicia couldn't respond.

"He took Frank's shirt? And that's why we're chasing after him like we're in some action movie? That's crazy!"

Without taking her eyes off the road, hoping to catch a glimpse of Hwang Tam's car up ahead of them, Teri replied, "It's the shirt that Frank was wearing when he was killed," a catch in her voice made her next words almost impossible to understand, but Felicia did, "it has his blood soaked into it. I can only touch him now by touching the blood still in his shirt."

Teri turned to face Felicia, "I have to get it back."

"The road! Keep your eyes on the road!" Felicia screamed as they rocketed past a tanker truck on its way to deliver gas to the service station in Kawaihae.

Teri turned her attention back to the road while Felicia tried to release her own white-knuckle grip on the dashboard.

CHAPTER FIFTY

Hwang Tam only slowed when he reached the turn for the airport. Even then his tires screeched as he rounded the corner and headed down the straightaway that led to the Kona International Airport. Behind him yellow rays of the sun struggled to push over the top of the mountains. He shot past the turn to the rental car facilities. He had no intention of turning the car in there.

Swinging right Hwang Tam followed the road around to the front of the low-lying terminal. He pulled in at the end of a line of three cars and one pickup truck that were offloading people and luggage.

Popping the trunk and leaving the keys in the ignition, Hwang Tam quickly retrieved his suitcase and the thick canvas golf carry-bag. He closed the trunk and set off down the sidewalk toward the terminal. He picked out the traffic officers whose job it was to keep people from parking overly long in the unloading zone. Hwang Tam fell in behind a group of three people hauling overloaded suitcases and backpacks toward the check-in area. One of the cars in line pulled away leaving a gap. Hwang Tam didn't look back, he walked on with confidence . . . right past the check-in area for United and on down toward the inter-island flights area.

He found a bench facing the roadway and sat down. Nonchalantly he shaded his eyes and looked first right and then left to see if his guide was there already. No. Hwang Tam blamed the sweat on his forehead on the increasing heat of the day and swiped at it with his handkerchief. One of the traffic officers was walking his way so Hwang Tam looked down at the ground at his feet. His heart froze when he noticed the blood splatters on his shoes.

"Hey, aloha, how you doing today?"

Hwang Tam looked up into the face of the traffic officer, standing right in front of him and partially blocking the rising sun behind him.

"I'm doing fine, officer."

"There's one car back there," the officer said as he indicated with a jerk of his head Hwang Tam's empty car. It stood out now that all the cars and the pickup in front of it had left the area. "Yours?"

"I don't drive, officer," Hwang Tam answered and he lifted the stub of his right hand as proof.

"Ooohh," said the officer. "So, sorry . . . sorry 'bout that."

"No," Hwang Tam explained, "I'm just waiting for my ride."

"Okay, have a nice day," and the officer walked off.

Hwang Tam's shirt was clinging to his body by now. He looked around again nervously and was rewarded by the sight of his guide pulling up to the curb in front of him.

Less than two minutes later the two men were pulling away from the curb, Hwang Tam's suitcase safely stored in the trunk of the beat-up old car . . . the thick canvas golf carry case riding on his lap.

An angry sun rose in the sky, its fiery rays following the two men as they headed south toward Hilo.

CHAPTER FIFTY-ONE

With Teri driving and Felicia hanging on for dear life the two women whipped around the corner and followed the same route that Hwang Tam had taken to the airport.

"There's the car!" Felicia exclaimed as she pointed out the rental car at the curb to Teri.

Teri pulled in right behind the car and the two women jumped out of Haunani's Highlander. They raced up, one on each side of the vehicle, only to pull back in disappointment. Empty!

"What now?" Felicia asked as they walked back to the Highlander.

Teri shook her head.

"Hey, you! You two! This your car?"

The traffic officer who called to them was the same one who had questioned Hwang Tam.

"No, not ours–" Teri stopped midsentence and pointed down the road.

"There he is!"

Felicia turned to look where Teri was pointing and was just able to catch a glimpse of Hwang Tam getting into some beat-up old car that immediately pulled away from the curb.

"Quick, let's go," Teri called to Felicia.

* * *

As the two women sped away in pursuit, the traffic officer shook his head, pulled out his pad and began copying down the license number and other information about the abandoned car. Somebody was going to pay big for this.

The ground shifted under his feet and his pen slipped on the citation pad in his hand. As the ground settled again the traffic officer looked up to the volcano.

What now, he thought, *the goddess restless again?*

CHAPTER FIFTY-TWO

After assuring his guide that he had the money, which he did not, Hwang Tam held on as they sped past the town of Kona and along the Queen Ka`ahumanu Highway. The Queen Ka`ahumanu soon became the Kuakini Highway and then the Mamalahoa Highway. Next they picked up the Hawai`i Belt Road, which they stayed on almost all the way out to Kurtistown. The closer they got to Hilo the heavier and denser the vog from the volcano became. The sulphur content of this local blend of fog and volcanic smoke was high today and began to affect the men's throats. Hwang Tam was relieved when his guide quickly swung off the main road and onto a paved one-lane road. Soon that gave way to a graveled road that very shortly died out. Now all they had to guide them were the ruts left by other vehicles. Ten minutes later his guide pulled to a stop and turned off the engine.

"Here we are," he announced pocketing the keys and climbing out his door.

Hwang Tam climbed out his side and stood looking around. He saw nothing.

"Here, this way," his guide directed and the two men set off on an almost-invisible trail through the undergrowth. The trail led to a rocky outcropping with a lava cave opening about seven feet high in the center of it. The opening was shielded from view by a number of tall thin trees.

"Okay, follow me an' watch your head . . . an' your feet," and without further instructions his guide pulled out a flashlight, clicked it on and proceeded to enter the dark forbidding lava cavern.

Hwang Tam followed, clutching the canvas golf carry bag.

* * *

The two men were so absorbed in their efforts that neither of them heard the low rumbling growl emitted by the volcano.

Teri and Felicia missed the turn and had to backtrack. Only the fact that the car they were pursuing had run through a puddle and left tracks going down the one-lane road kept them from losing Hwang Tam and his driver completely.

The two women arrived just minutes after the two men had entered the lava cavern. Teri felt that the seconds she spent digging out the flashlight Haunani kept in the Highlander for emergencies were wasted time, but it was necessary time. There was no way the two women could enter that pitch-black cavern without having some light to guide them.

They moved quickly trying to catch up to Hwang Tam and his driver. Once their eyes had adjusted to the darkness within, Teri spotted the flash from the men's flashlight ahead of them.

"Shhh," she cautioned Felicia and the two women proceeded as quietly as possible through the tomb-like atmosphere of the cavern.

CHAPTER FIFTY-THREE

Hwang Tam did his best to memorize the route they took through the lava tubes, just in case his guide proved untrustworthy. Even with his focus on what they were looking for, he was in awe of the striated colors of the flow stone in the tubes. At least he was until while looking at the walls of the current lava tube they were in he seriously barked his shin on a protuberance from the wall. After that he paid more attention to staying close to his guide and watching more carefully where he placed his feet.

* * *

Not all that far behind the two men, Teri and Felicia made their way as quietly as possible. Twice they had to stop and listen for the movements of the men in order to follow the correct path through the lava tubes. Teri kept her flashlight aimed down at the floor of the tube so as not to let the two men know that they were being followed.

* * *

Hwang Tam and his guide rounded a corner and, after a short distance, the guide stopped.

"We here."

"Where? I don't see anything."

In answer his guide shone his light at the wall on their right. Hwang Tam saw a gap in the wall with some rubble at its base. The opening was darker than any blackness Hwang Tam had ever seen.

"Come on," said his guide as he shone the light into the gap in the lava tube and stepped in.

Hwang Tam hesitated for only a moment before following him.

The guide stuck his flashlight into a crack in the lava, aiming it up so that the light bounced around the chamber making the items in there visible. Hwang Tam identified the basket he had seen in the photograph as well as the feathered god that stood next to it. The bones of a man, curled into a fetal position, at the feet of the small altar that the basket and god stood on did not affect him at all. Next to the skeleton lay a wicked looking lei o mano, formed from heavy Koa wood and lined all around with razor sharp shark's teeth.

But when he turned his head to the right and looked at the floor below the altar he froze. There lay the mummified body he had hoped to find. Moving quickly Hwang Tam knelt down beside the body and gingerly examined the silk robe. Old and precious. Folding the robe back from the body he did a brief examination; brief but enough to convince him that the man was Chinese. He had found his proof.

"Hey, professor, time for pay up."

Hwang Tam looked up at his guide standing beside him with his hand out. Reaching in his pocket Hwang Tam pulled out the roll of U.S. dollars that he had left.

"Here," he said pressing the money into his guide's hand while turning back to his examination of the mummified body.

"What's dis? Chump change? Hell, no more den one hundred dollars here. Where's da rest?"

"That's all I have left," Hwang Tam said.

"Das not enough fo' what I give you," the man said.

Hwang Tam turned as he heard a soft pop. He looked up to see the wiry man upend and pour some pungent liquid onto the mummified body. Hwang Tam quickly recognized the smell of some flammable liquid. His guide dropped the bottle and produced a butane lighter from his pocket.

"You bettah find mo' money in your pockets, or else I going torch dis guy."

"Wait, wait," Hwang Tam threw his left hand and right stump up in the air to ward off the threat, "I can get you more money. As soon as I get back to China –"

"Hell, I no wait for you . . . you get back to China you forget all about me," he flicked the lighter and the flame shot high.

Hwang Tam stumbled to his feet, "Let me . . . let me see," he said as he picked up the canvas golf carry bag from where he had dropped it upon entering the cave. Hwang Tam thrust his maimed arm into the bag and rummaged around.

"Here, you can have . . . THIS," and he whipped the bag across his guide's face. The wiry man fell back but didn't lose his grip on his lighter though the flame did go out.

"Son bitch," the man said turning back to the mummified body. He flicked the lighter again and held it with its jet of flame aloft.

In a panic Hwang Tam picked up the lei o mano with his left hand and swung it at the wiry man. He connected with the man's head. His guide fell like a rock onto the rough lava, blood pouring from a terrible gash in his head. His right ear was sliced off, flew through the air and landed in front of the feathered god statue. The lighter's flame extinguished as it struck the floor of the cave.

Seeing that the man didn't move, Hwang Tam quickly retrieved the canvas bag and proceeded to carefully lift and place the mummified body in it. He then rolled his guide over onto his back and took the car keys from his pocket. He was just about to retrieve the flashlight when he heard someone behind him.

"Hwang Tam!" Felicia's voice startled him.

"Keoki?" said Teri in surprise at seeing the hotel shuttle driver lying bleeding on the floor of the chamber.

Teri was almost all the way through the gap in the wall, while Felicia leaned in over her shoulder to take in the scene.

"What have you done?" Teri exclaimed.

Hwang Tam's eyes sped around the chamber and once more spotted the lei o mano lying on the floor where he had dropped it. He snatched it up again in his left hand, while all the while struggling to keep the canvas bag containing the mummified body tucked under his right armpit.

"I have found my proof! I have earned the right to be the head of the department at Beijing University! I have redeemed myself!" Hwang Tam raised the lei o mano again, "And no one is going to keep me from my destiny."

Reaching behind her Teri pushed Felicia back as Hwang Tam prepared to launch himself at the two women.

"Run, Felicia!" Teri screamed, and the two women took off up the lava tube away from the chamber. Unfortunately, they didn't run back the way they had come, but instead ran up the tube toward the spot where Lalepa had been killed.

Unwilling to leave his find behind, Hwang Tam was delayed in starting after the two women. It was difficult maneuvering out of the lava chamber while carrying the canvas bag with its contents. He found a strap on the bag that he could shove the stump of his right hand through and tucked Keoki's flashlight under his right arm. He still held the lei o mano in his left hand while he prepared to dispatch the two women. He could hear them not too far ahead and was sure they would not escape him.

* * *

Far down in the earth the volcano gave a slight hiccup. But that hiccup sent a gushing torrent of lava upwards. The hiccup also tore through a lava wall that for centuries had sealed off this lava tube from the rest of the lava field. Now nothing impeded the flow of the lava through the old tube. It rushed onward.

* * *

In the old bubble chamber Keoki woke to complete darkness. His head hurt horribly. He rolled onto his stomach and touched his head, his hand coming away wet and sticky.

"Son bitch hit me," he complained to no one in particular.

He realized that Hwang Tam had taken his flashlight and began to worry about how he would find his way out again without it to guide him.

Then Keoki noticed that the darkness was not so complete anymore. He could see things dimly in the chamber. Shadows flickered on the wall. Slowly he began to make out items in the cave. First he saw the ka'ai with its bones. Next he noticed the feathered god with his fierce grimace. Finally he observed an ear lying on the floor. He felt the side of his head and then reached out to pick up the ear. Holding it in his hand he looked back at the feathered god. It seemed as if the god statue wore a fierce smile now. The darkness fled as bright searing hot lava flooded the bubble chamber once more and wrapped Keoki in its fierce embrace cutting off his final cry of agony.

* * *

Teri and Felicia reached the end of the lava tube . . . and discovered that the way out there was impossible. Waves crashed on the rocks below and the climb down to those rocks was beyond their abilities.

"I saw some light through the roof just back a little ways," Felicia said.

Together they quickly retraced their steps. The lava tube here was tighter, rounder and only about seven feet in diameter. Up above in the roof of the tube that earlier hiccup had knocked some rocks loose and had opened a small hole overhead.

"Here, boost me up," Felicia told Teri.

Teri bent over and Felica stood on her back. Reaching up she was able to remove even more of the rocks from the opening.

"I think we can get through now," she said jumping down from Felicia's back.

"We better hurry," Teri replied as, looking down the tube, she saw the flash of Hwang Tam's light drawing nearer.

"You first," Teri said. Felicia opened her mouth and then saw that they didn't have time for an argument.

Teri cupped her hands and, pushing off Teri's shoulders, Felicia jumped for the opening. She missed the first time but managed to get first one, and then the other arm through on her second effort. She pulled herself up and out with great difficulty.

"I need to widen it a bit more," Felicia called down to Teri.

Teri stepped back as Felicia clawed and knocked more rocks out of the opening. Looking down the tube Teri saw Hwang Tam drawing even nearer.

"That's going to have to do," she called to Felicia.

"Stand on that big rock and see if you can jump up here," Felicia called down. She leaned down through the opening, dug her toes into the lava rock around her and stretched her arms out as far as she could.

Teri put one foot on the largest rock below the hole and used it to launch herself into the air. Felicia managed to grab Teri's right arm but missed her left. She quickly wrapped both hands around Teri's right hand and wrist. Teri brought her left hand up and grabbed onto Felicia's arm.

Felicia dragged herself backward while pulling Teri upward. Felicia thought her arms were going to come out of their sockets, but she refused to let go. Finally Teri was able to shove her left arm through the hole in the ceiling and grab onto the back of Felicia's pants. Teri was just finishing wriggling through the opening when Hwang Tam reached the spot below it.

Hwang Tam drew back his left arm to strike Teri's frantically thrashing legs with the lei o mano. Just as he made to strike the advancing lava flow reached a small puddle of water on the floor of the tube. The water disappeared in a puff of steam, but there was enough of it to cause the leading edge of the lava to spit out a tiny globule of molten rock. The bit of hot lava struck Hwang Tam on the thigh, burned through his pants immediately and charred a hole as big as the tip of an pencil eraser into his skin. The pain threw off his aim as he swung the lei o mano. The terrible weapon barely brushed Teri's right ankle. Even so the pain forced a scream from Teri's lungs.

Teri's scream urged Felicia to even greater efforts and she was delighted when Teri popped out of the hole like a cork from a bottle. Her joy was short-lived however when she saw the long gash in Teri's right ankle and the blood pouring from that wound.

"What now?" Felicia asked Teri.

"We run!" Teri said. "That madman just might find a way to get up here."

So they ran across the lava field, Felicia supporting Teri the whole way. Anyone observing them might have thought the two women were participating in a three-legged race. They were in a race, for the biggest prize of all. *Their lives!*

* * *

Hwang Tam screamed in frustration as Teri's lower body disappeared through the hole in the top of the lava tube. He picked up his flashlight from where he had dropped it and turned to try and retrace his steps out of the lava tube and back to the car he had arrived in. He had only taken a dozen or so steps when he felt the heat . . . and saw the lava flow rapidly moving up the tube toward him. There was no way around it.

He backed away from the oncoming lava, turned and, still carrying the mummified body, fled toward the light at the end of the tube. The options as he reached the opening to the sea did not look promising. But they were better than the options behind him.

Taking off his belt, Hwang Tam slipped it through the strap on the canvas bag, made sure the bag was securely zipped shut, and tied his belt around his chest. This allowed him to hold the canvas bag with the mummified body of the Captain in his arms. With one final look at the lava behind him Hwang Tam ran toward the opening and jumped as far out toward the water as he could.

He missed the rocks below by inches. The canvas bag stayed fastened to him and acted like a life preserver, bringing him back to the surface and supporting him in the midst of the waves.

Hwang Tam smiled broadly at his escape.

* * *

Down, far down below the surface of the earth, the volcano gave another little hiccup. The hiccup built up pressure behind the lava flow in the old tube and shot the molten lava out of the tube like water from a fire hose.

The thick stream of lava jetted out from the face of the cliff toward the ocean . . . engulfing Hwang Tam and the mummified body of treasure ship Captain Li Fong.

The waves crashed over them and hardened the lava almost immediately.

CHAPTER FIFTY-FOUR
Saturday, May 26, 2007

At first Felicia thought it was the small beam of sunlight coming through her bedroom window that dragged her back from her dreams. Then she thought that she must have heard someone moving past outside her room, and that was what woke her up. Whatever it was, she was awake now.

She looked down at her arms, the worst cuts covered with bandages, most of her injuries just scratches – red and angry-looking. She sat up and took inventory of her whole body. Bruises on her arms and legs were turning into technicolor wonders now.

Hearing some soft noises from outside her room again, Felicia swung her legs over the edge of the bed and got to her feet. She swayed, dizzy she guessed from sleeping so soundly. Her body ached all over. Retrieving her robe from the hook on the back of the door, she slipped it on, belted it and opened the door to the hallway corridor.

Felicia traced the noises to the front room of the house. There she found Haunani and Teri sitting at the dining table drinking coffee and reading the paper.

Upon her arrival both women jumped up and rushed over to hug Felicia. Teri had to hobble a bit, her right ankle wrapped in bandages. Teri, while hugging Felicia, repeated several times, "Thank you. Thank you so much."

Haunani stepped over to the Koa wood display table along the wall. Felicia was somewhat surprised to see the Ming Dynasty platter sitting in the center of the table, though she had vague memories of retrieving Hwang Tam's suitcase in the back of that old beat-up car that had been parked near the Highlander.

Haunani returned from the display table carrying a beautiful green lei which Felicia recognized as maile. Haunani draped the lei over Felicia's shoulders with the two ends of the lei hanging down in front.

"For you, Felicia. For saving my daughter."

"Thank you, Haunani," Felicia said. Playing with the two ends of the lei Felicia started to tie them together.

Haunani put her hand on Felicia's and stopped her.

"No, don't tie it. An old belief is that if a pregnant woman ties the ends of a lei together she might cause her baby's umbilical cord to knot."

"But I'm . . ." Felicia paused, looked at the two women standing there beaming with joy for her.

And just then the rich robust aroma of the fresh-brewed Kona coffee reached Felicia from the mugs on the dining table.

Her stomach rolled, turned a somersault and notified her of its intention to empty.

Felicia raced down the hall to the bathroom. She slammed the door shut behind her and flung her maile lei onto the towel rack. She barely had time to get down on her knees in front of the toilet before her vomiting started.

As she sat back on her heels after the first wave was through and waited for the second wave of nausea to strike her, Felicia was thankful that she had decided to get her hair cut short before this trip.

A Preview of the Next
Kohala Coast Thriller

THE OLD QUEEN'S SECRET

Felicia left the rental car with the valet and walked quickly through the lobby of the Queen's Beach Resort Hotel. Professor Thompson had paid the rental for the car upfront when the three of them had arrived on the island, and there were still three days left on the original contract. If it looked like her work wouldn't be wrapped up in that time Felicia assumed that she could always call and extend the contract on her credit card.

Leaving the lobby behind she made her way out to where the white sand beach replaced tile and concrete. Felicia kicked off her sandals and carried them in her hand as she made her way across the sand.

With the departure of her two colleagues, Felicia had been faced with a difficult decision. Should she return to Stanford University and resume work on her doctoral degree, or should she stay on the Big Island and attempt to complete the work begun by the archeological investigation team of which she had been a member.

She reasoned that even if she returned to Stanford now her work on her doctoral degree would still be delayed. But if she didn't return soon Jeremy, her fiancé, would miss her even more and would be longing for her return – she hoped.

If she stayed on the Big Island, even working alone, she should be able to complete the archeological investigation funded by the Queen's Beach Resort Hotel. And once she was finished the hotel could go ahead with their plans for the new tennis courts. Of course she wouldn't have been forced to work alone if not for the violent attack on one member of the investigation team, and the death of the other member. Then again, had circumstances been different she would have been the one buried on the island.

It was pleasant here on the Big Island, and she had bonded with Jeremy's sister Teri. But not so much with his mother, Haunani, or with his other sisters Lori and Shari. Felicia still felt a little uncomfortable staying at Jeremy's mother's house. It was as if Haunani was always watching her . . . and judging her. Trying to decide if Felicia was good enough for her son. Felicia knew that was a little unfair, but it was how she felt at times. Of course the morning sickness that she had been experiencing now for the past five days might be affecting her judgment as well. She wondered how Jeremy would react when she told him she was pregnant. She wondered even more how Haunani had known she was pregnant, even before she knew it herself.

Shaking her blonde hair, cut short to make it easier to deal with in the tropic heat and humidity, Felicia continued her walk across the white sand beach. This was her favorite time of day here on the islands, early morning with the sun just barely up in the sky. A light breeze on her face. All too soon the sun would begin to beat down upon her fair complexion, and unless she slathered the sunblock on she would feel, and show, the sun's effects later in the day.

Now she left the dry beach sand and walked along through the gently breaking surf. She enjoyed the feel of the warm tiny waves that covered her feet for a moment before withdrawing again. The tiny bubbles accompanying the waves tickled the tops of her feet.

One hundred yards down the beach Felicia was forced to leave the waves behind as she turned inland, mauka as she had learned to say in Hawai`ian, and headed toward the lawn area behind the white sand beach. Reaching the lawn she scuffed her feet through the rough grass in order to knock the clinging sand from her wet feet. When she had gotten most of the sand off Felicia replaced her sandals on her feet and headed toward the site of the archeological investigation.

A backhoe and a small tractor sat off to one side of a partially excavated area approximately one hundred and twenty feet long by seventy feet wide. It had been dug down to a depth of almost six feet over the whole site with a ramp dug out at one end to allow the two machines access. The excavation was roughly done since it had been halted not long after it was begun. Yellow *CAUTION* tape surrounded the whole excavation with signs posted stating *NO ENTRY – KAPU – AUTHORIZED PERSONNEL ONLY*. Felicia ducked under the tape and moved carefully across the site. She and the other members of the team had made a good start on their studies on the side nearest the ocean. Today she was going to work on the mauka side of the excavation, the side that would remain in the shade for quite some time. By the time the sun struck that area Felicia hoped to be finished for the day.

Pausing in the middle of the excavation, Felicia picked up a screening pan about eighteen inches across, a small hand hoe, a two-foot long metal rod, a long-handled brush, a wide paintbrush and a narrow paintbrush. She continued on into the cooling shade of the overhanging palm trees. After regarding the area for a minute Felicia picked a place to start work for the day.

She hadn't been working more than five minutes before she turned up a pelvic bone along with femur and a tibia. As an archeologist Felicia was delighted by these discoveries rather than horrified. She took a small notebook and ballpoint pen from the back pocket of her baggy shorts and made a few notes with the pen. Then, with a permanent black marker, also residing in her back pocket, she wrote identifying numbers on each bone. She carefully placed the bones off to the side for now.

As she prepared to return to her exploration of this area of the excavation, Felicia noticed that the dirt in the shadow toward the edge of the excavation looked a little different. It looked almost as if the ground there had been dug up sometime prior to now and then filled back in. Her curiosity aroused Felicia stepped carefully over to that area and knelt down. Probing the ground with the rod Felicia found resistance only a few inches below the surface. She began to carefully remove the dirt there. Her heart beat faster as the outline of a skull began to take shape. Another body! This definitely was a burial ground of ancient Hawai`ian remains, iwi as the Hawai`ians called them. Once Felicia had identified all of the remains, and she thought

3

she was close to that point now, there would only be the matter to be decided as to what to do with those remains. The options being to rebury them here, under this proposed tennis court, or to rebury them elsewhere. In either case a Hawaiian priest would be needed to consecrate their burial site.

So engrossed in thinking about the whole process she was involved in, Felicia had been digging mechanically and had not paid full attention to the skull she was uncovering. Focusing in on the now mostly-exposed skull Felicia jumped backwards and wound up sitting in the dirt staring at the skull.

It was not the type of skull she was used to finding. This one had hair . . . and dried skin . . . and eye sockets that, even though sightless, seemed to cry out to Felicia for help. As the sandy soil clinging to the front of the skull fell away Felicia turned away. The bile rose in her throat at the sight of the skull's empty mouth. Empty because someone had smashed out all the teeth from the mouth leaving behind only shredded and torn lips and gums.

This was no anonymous ancient dead person . . . this was a recent murder victim.

More Books by The Author

The Bones of the Kuhina Nui

First book in the Kohala Coast Thriller Series.

The Old Queen's Murder

Second book in the Kohala Coast Thriller Series.

Primo's: The Kaua'i Obake Bar

First book in the Primo series. Humorous and spooky short stories set in and around a bar in the town of Kapaa on the island of Kaua'i in the early 1970's.

Is 'Chicken Skin' a Local Delicacy?

Second book in the Primo series. More adventures with the gang from Primo's Bar.